"I can't be yo[u]
and survive, [...]

Her words rang w[ith honesty.] If anything remains of the love you said you felt for me, you'll let me go."

He stood up, a muscle clenching in his square jaw. His voice was as low as hers had been when he said, "If anything remains? Hell, Miriam, you've got no idea, have you?"

"Don't—don't do this."

"What? This?" He pulled her up and into his arms, kissing her hard.

HELEN BROOKS lives in Northamptonshire, and is married with three children and three beautiful grandchildren. As she is a committed Christian, busy housewife, mother and grandma, her spare time is at a premium, but her hobbies include reading, swimming and gardening, and walks with her husband and their Irish terrier. Her long-cherished aspiration to write became a reality when she put pen to paper on reaching the age of forty and sent the result off to Harlequin.

THE MILLIONAIRE'S CHRISTMAS WIFE

HELEN BROOKS

~ SNOW, SATIN AND SEDUCTION ~

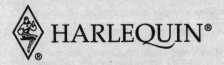

TORONTO • NEW YORK • LONDON
AMSTERDAM • PARIS • SYDNEY • HAMBURG
STOCKHOLM • ATHENS • TOKYO • MILAN • MADRID
PRAGUE • WARSAW • BUDAPEST • AUCKLAND

Recycling programs
for this product may
not exist in your area.

ISBN-13: 978-0-373-52741-0

THE MILLIONAIRE'S CHRISTMAS WIFE

First North American Publication 2009.

Copyright © 2009 by Helen Brooks.

www.eHarlequin.com

Printed in U.S.A.

THE MILLIONAIRE'S
CHRISTMAS WIFE

CHAPTER ONE

'ONLY eight weeks till Christmas. Have you decided when you're going to come up and join us all? I thought it might be nice if you tried to make it on Christmas Eve and then stayed over for the New Year.'

Her mother's voice held the sort of briskness that said she wasn't going to take no for an answer. Miriam knew she meant well but the thought of spending several days with her mother and other well-meaning relatives and old friends verged on nightmarish. Everyone would be thinking about what happened at Christmas last year and being intensely careful not to mention it. Or ask any personal questions. Or behave naturally.

Miriam took a deep breath. 'I'm sorry but I shan't be around this Christmas.'

'Won't be around?' Anne Brown's voice sharpened. 'What does that mean? You're not going to sit and mope in that awful little bedsit, are you?'

'It's not an awful little bedsit and no, I'm not going to sit and mope. I'm going to Switzerland, as it happens. Skiing.'

'*Skiing?*' Her mother's voice was so shrill Miriam winced and held the phone away from her ear. 'You can't ski.'

'I'm going to learn,' Miriam said patiently.

'When was this decided?'

'Clara and I got our tickets yesterday.'

'Clara? I might have known she'd be at the bottom of this.' Now her mother's voice was overtly hostile.

Enough was enough. 'Actually it was me who mentioned to Clara at the weekend what I was going to do, and she asked if she could come along. I think it was because she feels like you and doesn't want me to be without company at Christmas.' Miriam's voice had an edge to it. Her mother had only met Clara once on the day Miriam had moved into the bedsit in Kensington, but the other girl's mauve spiky hair, panda eye make-up and Gothic clothes, not to mention her numerous piercings, had labelled her a bad influence as far as Anne was concerned. In truth Clara was one of the funniest, most sweet-natured and generous people Miriam had ever met, and she didn't know how she would have got through the past ten months without her.

Her mother sniffed. Eloquently. 'Well, you would say that, wouldn't you? Does Jay know you're thinking of spending Christmas in Switzerland?'

Don't lose your temper. She loves you and she's concerned, besides which you don't want her to do the wobbly-voiced long-suffering-mother routine. Forcing a calmness she didn't feel into her voice, Miriam said measuredly, 'Why would Jay know what I'm doing or not doing, Mother?'

'Because he's your husband, of course.'

'In name only.' She took a deep breath. 'And you might as well know I'm going to ask him for a divorce soon.' She didn't know why she hadn't done it before except she hadn't wanted to contact him and face all the hoo-ha that would result. It had been easier to pretend he didn't exist while she licked her wounds and attempted to regain her equilibrium. Which she had done now. She was much, much better, she assured herself silently. Back to normal really.

'So you're still determined not to believe him?'

How many times had they had this conversation since the day she had walked out of her beautiful marital home and into the bedsit? Too many. Miriam's voice reflected this when she said, 'This conversation's going nowhere and I'm late for an appointment. I'll ring you at the weekend, OK? Love you.'

She turned off her mobile. Her mother wouldn't like it, of course, but it would be her poor stepfather who would have to put up with the martyr attitude that would invariably follow. The 'I've got the most ungrateful and stubborn daughter in the world' scenario.

Miriam shut her eyes tightly for a moment. She didn't understand—and would never understand—how her mother could still continue to regard Jay as the best thing since sliced bread after what he'd done. But then after one glance from his tawny-brown eyes most women were putty in Jay's hands. As she had been. Once.

Her mouth firming, Miriam picked up her keys and exited the bedsit after one glance round the bright, uncluttered room. It might, in all honesty, have been termed awful when she had first seen it on a bleak wintry day at the beginning of the year, she acknowledged, descending the steep stairs to Clara's bedsit on the bottom floor of the three-storeyed Victorian terrace. But plenty of elbow grease, several tins of paint, new laminate flooring and her own furniture had transformed the place.

It was her tiny sanctuary, she told herself, pausing outside Clara's room. Her cream sofa converted to a bed at night, and her bistro table and chairs set by the large window afforded a panoramic view over London rooftops and the wide expanse of sky above that never ceased to thrill her, night and day. The minute kitchen area in one corner served culinary needs fairly adequately, and the built-in wardrobe and cupboards along one wall—now painted barley-white—meant the room was always spick and span without stuff lying about. She'd learnt very quickly that even a jumper or jacket draped over a chair made the compact space appear untidy.

She knocked on Clara's door. They cooked each other dinner now and again and tonight was Clara's turn, but she didn't think her mother would have appreciated knowing what her 'appointment' entailed.

The door opened immediately. 'You're bang on time as always,' Clara said with a note of amazement. Punctuality wasn't Clara's strong point. Nor was tidiness, Miriam reflected, picking her way over the floor, which was strewn with clothes, magazines, shoes and umpteen other things, to the kitchen area.

'Something smells fantastic.' It was one of Clara's quirks that she could take a load of ingredients and seemingly fling them together and they always came out utterly delicious. 'What are we having?'

Clara wrinkled her snub nose. 'I'd got nothing in so it's onion and mustard mash with sausages; nothing special. Help yourself to a glass of wine,' she added, inclining her head at the opened bottle on the tiny breakfast bar which separated the kitchen from the rest of the room. 'It's a good one. Dave brought it the other night.'

Since Miriam had known the other girl Clara had had a number of boyfriends, none of whom lasted for more than a month on average. As soon as Clara had got them interested she got bored and yet another hopeful beau was shown the door. The fact that they all fell madly in love with her seemed to be the death knell as far as Miriam could make out. It wasn't that Clara was shallow exactly, but once the challenge was gone, so was Clara. Dave was two weeks strong at the moment but already a note of disinterest had crept into Clara's voice.

Miriam eyed her friend. 'You're going off him, aren't you?' she accused mildly. 'Don't tell me he's talking about for ever already?'

Clara giggled. 'He wants me to meet his mother,' she admitted. 'I mean, can you imagine *me* meeting anyone's mother? They'd die of shock.'

Miriam smiled as she was meant to but inside she found herself envying Clara's carefree approach to life and love. They were so different, she thought as she sipped at the wine—which was a *very* good one—but perhaps that was why they hit it off so well. Clara was the original free spirit, which was reflected in the way she looked and the clothes she wore; *she,* on the other hand, had aspired to be nothing more than a wife and mother since she was a little girl playing with her dolls. Clara was a television researcher, a job that was as varied as it was hard work, and she was brilliant at it. *She* was secretary to a successful lawyer and loved the fact her job was nine-to-five with no hidden panics or surprises. Clara was quicksilver, she was quiescent, which was probably why Jay had strayed so early in their marriage, she told herself broodingly. She was too dull, too uninteresting to hold a man like Jay Carter.

'You're thinking of him again, aren't you?' Clara said

suddenly. 'I can always tell. You get this haunted look. Has he phoned again?'

Miriam shook her head.

'Written?'

'No, we haven't been in contact since the spring.'

'Was that the time you told him you loathed even the thought of him and wished you'd never set eyes on him?'

Clara's memory was too good sometimes. She hadn't felt proud of that last conversation when she had said far too much. 'Uh-huh,' she mumbled, taking a big gulp of wine.

'Then what's prompted the face?'

'I can't help my face,' Miriam said reasonably. And when Clara just raised one pierced eyebrow and waited, she added reluctantly, 'My mother phoned and I told her about Christmas.'

'Ah…' Clara dished up two platefuls of fragrant, steaming mash and added three fat, done-to-a-turn sausages per plate. 'And she asked if you had told Jay you were spending Christmas with the wild witch of the west, and you told her it was none of Jay's business.'

It was moments like this that revealed why Clara was so highly regarded in the career she'd chosen, despite her outward nonconformity. Under the mauve hair was an acutely intelligent and discerning mind. 'Something like that,' Miriam murmured.

'Right. We're going to finish this bottle and open another and forget all about men. OK?' Clara's blue eyes held Miriam's soft brown ones. 'And then we're going to talk about Switzerland and what clothes we need to buy for the evenings with all those gorgeous men about.'

'I thought we were going to forget about men.'

'Only the ones in the past and present. The future is

something else. Oh, no, I've just thought of something. I can't go to Switzerland.'

Miriam sat up straighter at the note of alarm in Clara's voice. 'Why not?'

'How is Father Christmas going to fill my stocking if I'm in a different country?'

'You're a nut.' Miriam smiled, nudging Clara with her elbow. But a very nice nut.

It was gone ten o'clock when Miriam climbed the stairs to her bedsit and she was in a far better frame of mind than when she'd left it earlier. Clara was a tonic, she thought, smiling to herself as she let herself into the room and switched on the lights. She had left her mobile in the bedsit because she hadn't been able to face the thought of talking to her mother again that night, but as she passed it her conscience took over and she picked it up to check her messages.

There were two. The first one was from her mother, as she had expected, terse and to the point, saying of course Miriam must do as she wanted with regard to Christmas but everyone was going to be terribly disappointed not to see her, and with Great-Aunt Abigail's health being so poor it might be the old lady's last Christmas.

Miriam wrinkled her nose. Emotional blackmail. Her mother was a dab hand at it. But, considering she had never liked Great-Aunt Abigail and Great-Aunt Abigail had never liked her, she didn't think her absence would cause too many tears.

She pressed the button for the next call. 'Hello, Miriam.' Jay's deep, smoky voice was the same one that featured in her dreams far too often for her liking. 'I think we've got things to discuss, don't you? I'm not prepared for this state of affairs to continue any longer and, in spite of the fact that you don't want to be on the same planet as me, I suggest we tackle this as adults rather than petulant children. I'll call again if you don't call back. Just so you know. Goodbye for now.'

Miriam sat down very suddenly. Jay. For a moment all she could do was repeat his name in her head. Taking hold of her whirling emotions, she forced herself to listen to the message again, and this time the cold, businesslike tone to his voice registered.

He had turned up unexpectedly a couple of times since the day she had left him and phoned frequently until the day in the spring when she knew she had mortally offended him, but never in all their dealings had his voice carried such an icy chill to it. It seemed she wouldn't have to be the one to instigate divorce proceedings after all, she told herself sickly. It sounded as though he was ringing to set that particular ball in motion himself. Of course, she could be wrong. Bitter experience was proof she didn't have a clue what made Jay Carter tick.

Rising to her feet, she walked across the room and made herself a cup of hot chocolate. She needed something to combat the butterflies in her stomach. Then she dialled Jay's number.

'Hello?'

The butterflies ignored the soothing effects of the hot chocolate and instead went for gold in the fluttering stakes. Swallowing hard, Miriam said, 'Hello, Jay. You wanted to talk to me?'

'Miriam?'

He knew jolly well it was her. 'Yes,' she said, her voice clipped now. 'I've been out.'

'Does that mean you didn't take your phone with you or you were too…busy to answer it when it rang?'

It was nothing to do with him either way. Ignoring the question, she repeated stonily, 'You wanted to talk to me?'

'I think we *need* to talk,' he corrected silkily.

Miriam blinked. The snub had been delivered with a smooth flatness but was a snub none the less. Recovering immediately, she said coolly, 'So talk.'

'Oh, no, Miriam. This time we do it my way. Civilised, over a meal and a drink. That's what grown-up people do.'

Her temper was slowly chasing away the last of the butterflies. 'Really? I take it this is in the same realm as adultery being an accepted social pastime for "grown-up" men and women?'

There was a pregnant pause before he said, 'I'll ignore that. Tomorrow night. Are you free?'

She was but not for the world would she have admitted it. 'Sorry, already booked.'

'OK, we could go on like this for hours. When are you able to have dinner with me?'

Ridiculous, because he was only talking about dinner, but his dark, smoky voice was having an unwelcome effect on her equilibrium. Or perhaps it wasn't so much her mental or emotional equanimity, she admitted with hot shame, as a throbbing warmth spread throughout her lower stomach. How she could still physically want him after what he had done she didn't know, but it appeared her body was working independently to the rest of her. 'Let me see…' She allowed a moment or two to pass, more to gain control over her voice than anything else. A breathless stammer just wasn't an option.

Today was Tuesday. 'Friday?' she said as steadily as she

could, considering her whole body was quivering with something she labelled lust.

'Yep, Friday's good for me.'

He sounded insultingly relaxed about the wait, she noted with a mixture of hurt and bitterness. But then she had no doubt at all Jay could fill his evenings without any trouble whatsoever. From the first day she had met him she had known women found him totally irresistible. 'Fine, Friday it is.'

'I'll pick you up at eight.'

Now he had got his own way he sounded almost uninterested, but then that was the nature of the beast, Miriam told herself silently. Jay was the ultimate alpha male, the leader, the hunter. How she could have been so incredibly stupid as to get mixed up with him in the first place she still didn't know, but she had further compounded that mistake by believing him when he'd said he loved her and wanted her to marry him, that the two of them would be a forever witness to the power of true love. Her thoughts prompted her to say, 'Wouldn't it be better to communicate through our solicitors? I mean, we've said all we can say, surely?'

'Perhaps.' It was cold. Chilling. 'But I'll pick you up at eight.'

The kicked-in-the-stomach feeling she was experiencing didn't give her any strength to argue. Suddenly a sense of fatalism was there. Maybe she had to go through the final death throes to emerge whole again, she thought a trifle hysterically. 'You—you've got my address?'

'I know where you live, Miriam.'

'Oh, right.'

'Goodnight.'

When the phone went dead she continued to stare at it blankly for a moment or two. That was it. End of conversation. He had got what he wanted and so there was no need to prolong what had probably been to him a tedious exchange. 'I hate you,' she whispered into the silent room. She did, she *really* hated him.

But did she hate him enough? a separate part of her mind asked disturbingly. Enough to remain strong when they met, enough to refuse to let him walk all over her, enough to show him that she was finished with him for good?

Reaching for the last of the hot chocolate, she drained the mug and rose to her feet. She wasn't going to do this—the endless soul-searching that she'd indulged in for so long in the caustic aftermath of their separation. It got her nowhere. Facts were what mattered. Jay had slept with another woman just six months after he had stood at the altar and promised to love, honour and cherish *her*. End of story.

Her mouth pulled tight with pain, Miriam placed the empty mug in the tiny sink in the kitchen area and walked over to the sofa. The beginnings of a headache drummed a persistent tattoo at the backs of her eyes and she pressed her fingers into the side of her forehead.

Perhaps it was as well Jay had phoned tonight, she told herself as she swiftly converted the sofa into a snug bed and got undressed. Once in her nightie she padded along to the bathroom at the end of the landing which she shared with the other occupant of that floor, a young student called Caroline, who was rarely at home since she'd found a boyfriend with his own flat. After a perfunctory wash she brushed her teeth and went back to her room, her mind still gnawing over the events of the last half-hour. Yes, all things considered, Jay contacting her wasn't necessarily a bad thing. He was right, they couldn't go on as they were, in a state of limbo. Their marriage was over and the sooner it was made legally so, the better. He had never been right for her; from the beginning she had known she was out of his league. He was far more suited to a woman like Belinda Poppins.

Poppins. She made a sound in the back of her throat. If ever a woman had been misnamed, Belinda had. She was as unlike a magical nanny who made everything all right for everyone she came into contact with as it was possible to be. Tall and elegant, with a perfect figure that looked sensational in anything and everything, Belinda was the sort of private secretary that was every wife's worst nightmare. The original man-eater.

Miriam stood for a moment in front of the full-length mirror in the bedsit, surveying her reflection critically. Soft brown eyes set in an oval face liberally sprinkled with freckles stared back at her, her shoulder-length chestnut hair and creamy skin completing a picture of gentle benevolence. She was the sort of person babies and animals liked instinctively, her aura of innocent non-aggression drawing any waif and stray within a fifty-mile radius to her side. Most of her boyfriends before she'd met Jay had had something of the lame duck about them once she'd got to know them; she seemed to attract such types. And then Jay Carter had blazed into her life.

She jerked away from the mirror, telling herself to stop thinking about him, but her mind was set on a certain course now and the memories were flooding in.

She'd met him on a wild, windy March afternoon in the middle of a torrential downpour when her umbrella had chosen to turn itself inside out. She'd cannoned straight into him, the force of his hard, unyielding male body almost knocking her over but for his arms coming out to grab her. Corny, but it had been love at first sight. At least for her, she thought miserably, climbing into bed and pulling the duvet up to her chin. With hindsight she now saw, whatever he'd felt for her, it hadn't been the love she'd believed it was.

They had married three months later after a whirlwind romance during which she'd lived on cloud nine, unable to believe a man like Jay—a wealthy, successful, handsome and charismatic entrepreneur with the Midas touch—wanted *her*, Miriam Brown. They had honeymooned for a month in Italy at the beautiful villa set in the hills that Jay had bought some years before, before returning home to his palatial apartment in Westminster which overlooked the river.

She had continued at her job in the law firm, not because she had to—Jay was rich enough for her never to work again—but because she wanted to. The thought of sitting at home all day twiddling her thumbs or becoming one of the 'lunch' crowd who drank g & ts, nibbled on lettuce leaves and then shopped all afternoon filled her with horror. Once she was expecting a baby she'd consider giving in her notice, she'd decided, but until then she'd carry on as before. Although now, instead of going home to the flat she had shared with three other girls she'd been at university with, she had Jay.

She had been so looking forward to their first Christmas together. Much to Jay's amusement she'd spent a fortune on Christmas decorations in November and on the first weekend in December had turned the apartment into a vision of gold and red, transforming its rather masculine decor of coffee and dark browns mixed with off-white.

As a child her Christmases had, of necessity, been frugal

affairs, her father having walked out on her mother and herself when she was six years old, leaving behind a mass of debt. He had disappeared off to some foreign destination with the woman he'd been seeing on the quiet, leaving her mother to pick up the pieces of their shattered life as best she could. They hadn't seen him from that day to the time, ten years later, her mother had been notified of his death in a car accident. Her mother had remarried a year later.

Miriam turned over in bed, irritable and annoyed with herself for the trip down memory lane. She didn't want to think about her father or Jay—they were two of a kind, she told herself bitterly. Egotistical and self-centred, the sort of men who would never be satisfied with one woman for long. She had always been amazed at her mother's lack of bitterness where her father was concerned; she'd never spoken ill of him, not even through the years when they'd lived in one flea-bitten dump after another, struggling to get by on what her mother earned as a dental nurse. She'd known, deep inside, that her mother still loved him, even though they'd never spoken of it. It was only after her mother knew he was dead that she ceased to give up hoping he'd come back. Then she'd begun to live again.

Well, she didn't intend to waste years of her life doing the same thing with regard to Jay. The old adage of 'like mother, like daughter' wasn't an option in this case, Miriam thought darkly. She sat up in bed and gave her pillow a series of thumps. It felt as if it had bricks in it. Lying down again, she stared, unseeing, in the darkness.

Would she have found out about Jay and Belinda if she hadn't gone to his office the night before Christmas Eve when she had finished work early after the law firm's Christmas party? She had to admit she had never liked the other woman from the day she'd met her shortly after she had first started seeing Jay. They'd bumped into Belinda and a man friend at the theatre one evening and she had noticed then the way Jay's secretary had looked at him with hungry eyes. Perhaps it was from that point her unease about Belinda had begun to make itself felt. But she had trusted Jay then. Believed him when he said she was the only woman in the world for him and he would love her for ever and ever.

Full of the plans for the big Christmas Eve dinner party they were giving for family and a few close friends, she had sailed up to his office on the top floor of Carter Enterprises with nothing more on her mind than whether to ask the caterers to cut the Christmas cake before or during the coffee and brandy stage of the meal. Jay had held his firm's Christmas party that afternoon too and most of the employees had already left, but there had been a light burning in his office as she had walked along the thickly carpeted corridor.

She'd entered noiselessly and so had seen them before they had seen her. Jay had been standing with his back to her, jacketless and with the sleeves of his shirt rolled up, and Belinda had been perched on the edge of his desk, her tight skirt riding up high over her thighs and the buttons of her blouse undone, revealing the skimpiest of lace bras which did nothing to hide her voluptuous breasts. Belinda's eyes had flicked towards her and whether it was that or whether she had made a sound herself Miriam didn't know, but suddenly Jay had swung round and saw her.

'Miriam!' As she had turned to run, his voice had cut through the air. 'Wait, this isn't what you think.'

She had reached the lift when he caught her, his hands

fastening on her forearms as he had moved her to face him. 'Listen to me,' he'd said urgently. 'Let me explain.'

'I don't want you to explain.' She had been beside herself with shock and pain. 'I saw enough to know exactly what was happening.'

'You don't, that's what I'm trying to say. Listen, I didn't know she was there—'

'She's *your* secretary, in *your* office, half-dressed and you didn't know she was there?' she'd all but screamed at him. 'Surely you can come up with something better than that?'

'It's the truth. I'd been working and gone to get myself a coffee—'

'Since when do you get your own coffees?'

'Since everyone's gone home for Christmas.'

'Not everyone, Jay,' she'd shot back, incensed he could think she was so gullible. 'You're here and so is she. If you wanted a coffee, couldn't Belinda have got it?'

'I thought she'd left with the others.'

'And you're telling me you came back and there she was, lying over your desk with her skirt up round her ears and everything on offer?'

Belinda had appeared behind Jay at that moment, her blouse fastened and not a hair out of place as she had purred, 'Miriam, I'm so sorry,' as her feline eyes had glittered with satisfaction.

'No, you're not.' She'd stared straight into the carefully made-up face. 'You're not sorry at all. You've always wanted him, haven't you? Well, be my guest. He's all yours.'

The lift had opened right on cue and she had stepped into it, Jay following her a second later. As the doors closed Belinda stood watching them, her face impassive, but the green-flecked eyes narrowed on Jay as he said, 'You're not going like this, not until I tell you what happened. Surely you don't think for one moment I want her?'

She had actually put her hands over her ears at that point. 'Don't treat me as though I'm as foolish as my mother, Jay, because I'm not. I saw what I saw.' As he had reached out to touch her she had slapped his hand away with some force. 'Don't, don't you dare,' she'd shouted, on the verge of hysterics. 'I never want you to touch me again.'

'Stop this.' His face had been white and shocked but now he was getting angry too, his voice harsh as he'd ground out, 'I'm asking you to let me explain.'

'And I'm telling you I don't want to hear.' The lift doors glided open in Reception and now she lowered her voice, aware of the one remaining receptionist on duty as she said, 'I suggest you get back to her because I don't want you.'

'This is ridiculous.'

'Ridiculous or not, that's the way I feel.'

'I'll take you home. Wait while I get my jacket.'

'I'm not waiting for you, Jay. I thought you knew me well enough to understand that word doesn't feature in my vocabulary. I watched my mother waiting for my father for years and years.'

'You're being unreasonable. I'm asking you, *telling* you to wait here for two minutes while I get my jacket, OK? If you're not here when I get down there'll be hell to pay, Miriam. I mean it. We're going to talk this through and it's not going to ruin our Christmas.'

Ruin their Christmas? She stared at him with huge eyes. Was he mad? She'd just caught him with another woman and he was talking about ruining their Christmas? What about the rest of their lives?

As soon as he had disappeared into the lift she left the

building, hailing a taxi which had—miraculously in the circumstances—passed by empty. Once in the apartment she threw a few things into a suitcase, work-ing purely on automatic and praying all the time Jay wouldn't arrive before she had left. She had just exited the apartment block and crossed the road when a taxi screeched to a halt outside the building. Melting into the shadows, she watched as Jay leapt out of the car. It had been too dark to see his face clearly but she hadn't had to to know he was furiously angry. It was evident in every line of his body.

Once he had gone inside she had made her escape. She hadn't gone to her mother and stepfather, knowing that was the first place he'd try, but instead had booked into a hotel for the night. From there she had phoned her mother and told them the dinner party on Christmas Eve was off and why, and asked her to let everyone know. It was only when her mother had become somewhat tearful that she'd promised she'd go and see them the next day and stay over Christmas. Then she had had a long hot bath and cried enough tears to fill it twice over before falling asleep exhausted at some point in the evening.

When Jay had turned up at her mother's the next day she hadn't been surprised; he'd been phoning her mobile every few minutes but she hadn't taken the calls. He'd given the same explanation, adding Belinda had had too much to drink at the Christmas party, which was why she'd acted as she had. He wasn't excusing her, he'd said crisply, but apparently she'd gone to sleep in an empty office somewhere and then arrived in his while he was getting himself the coffee. He had walked in to find her reclining on his desk, half-undressed. She could believe him or not, but that was the truth. She'd said she chose not to believe him and he had left after telling her not to be such a little fool and to take time to think logically. He wasn't going to beg and plead, he'd added. Trust was an essential ingredient in any marriage and it was about time she grew up and realised that.

His attitude had shaken her. He had seemed so staunch in what he said, totally unwavering in his explanation of what had happened. By the time she'd returned to work after the Christmas break—the worst time of her life—she had been weakening. Her mother had been insistent she'd made the biggest mistake of her life in walking out on Jay and—mainly, Miriam admitted, because she badly wanted to believe his version of events—she'd begun to think she might have got it wrong.

Then on that first morning back at work Belinda had phoned her.

Miriam sat up in bed. This was ridiculous. She was never going to be able to sleep now and why she was doing a post-mortem at this late stage she didn't know. Everything was cut and dried and had been for ages. She had made her decision in January and it was irrevocable.

Switching on the light, she reached for a book on the table next to the sofa bed. She read a couple of pages without taking a word in; all she could focus on was the memory of Belinda's sugary-sweet voice on that morn-ing ten months ago.

She was so sorry, Belinda had murmured, that Miriam had had to find out about the affair the way she had, but she must believe it was over now. She wasn't returning to work at Carter Enterprises—she had left Jay's employ—so there was no chance temptation could rear its head again.

Miriam had listened, sickened, as the soft voice had gone on. With the benefit of hindsight she realised she should have put the phone down as soon as Belinda had spoken, but she had been like a rabbit immobilised and horribly fascinated in the glare of the headlights of the car that was going to destroy it.

She just wanted to explain, Belinda had gone on, that she didn't make a habit of sleeping with married men but, as Miriam had probably realised by now, Jay was irresistible when he wanted something. She'd fallen madly in love with him even though she had known deep down that for him it was only a physical thing and that he was the sort of man who would always take advantage of the attraction he held for women. But she did wish Miriam well...

She *had* put the phone down at this point but it had been too late. Belinda's words had burnt themselves like a branding iron into her mind. She had known then that her marriage was over.

Of course, Jay had denied everything when she'd told him what Belinda had said later that day when he had called her to ask when she was returning home. Belinda was a woman scorned, he'd insisted. When he had told her there was no way they could work together again after what had happened she had become abusive, threatening all sorts of repercussions. This was her revenge for his rejection of her. It was perfectly obvious, wasn't it? Transparent, even.

The conversation had rapidly developed into a full-scale row with things said on both sides that would have been better unsaid. In the end she had told him she was going to see about getting somewhere else to live in the morning; she wouldn't be returning to the apartment. Ever. There had been a long pause and then his voice had been quiet, almost conversational, when he had said, 'You must do as you see fit, Miriam. Whatever I thought we had, I was mistaken. You've never loved me, not if you're prepared to bail out the first time we hit a problem.'

It had been the final straw. 'A problem?' she'd screamed down the phone. 'A *problem* is leaving the top off the toothpaste every morning or forgetting a birthday or not cleaning the bath properly after you've used it. This isn't a problem, Jay. This is a third person in our marriage and it's one too many for me.'

'You don't trust me. You're prepared to take Belinda's word against mine. Damn it, you *want* to believe her.'

Maybe the harsh note of anger and resentment in his voice should have warned her. 'If that's the way you want to look at it,' she'd replied, feeling as though she was dying inside.

'Then perhaps some time apart is best. When you're prepared to at least listen to what I have to say, contact me.' And he'd put the phone down. Just like that.

Miriam slung the book to one side. Sliding out of bed, she fixed herself another mug of hot chocolate and took a couple of aspirin for the headache, switching the TV on and watching an old comedy programme while she drank.

It was nearly an hour later before she settled down in bed again and this time, with the help of the aspirin and not least because she was emotionally exhausted, she fell straight to sleep.

CHAPTER TWO

'ARE you sure you're doing the right thing? I could come with you if you like; your ex wouldn't frighten me.'

Miriam smiled at Clara. 'You haven't met Jay.'

'I don't have to meet him to know that.' Clara grinned. The day before she had dyed her hair a bright fuchsia red, leaving a halo of purple round her face. The effect was extraordinary. 'I haven't come across one of the male species yet who frightens me. It's usually the other way round if anything.'

'Thanks, but it's better I get this over and done with as quickly as possible and without antagonising him before a word's said.'

Clara nodded. 'As long as you're up to it.'

Up to it? Never in a hundred years. 'Course I am,' Miriam said brightly.

'You ought to make it clear you're going to take him for every penny you can get,' the normally unmaterialistic Clara said darkly. 'The rat.'

'I don't want his money,' said Miriam simply. 'I just want out with the minimum of fuss.' She still felt too bruised, too sore to engage in a fight over who had what. Besides, she had brought nothing into the marriage; all the wealth was Jay's and he could keep it.

Clara surveyed her under kohl-blackened lids. 'He's an idiot to have lost you.'

'He doesn't think so.'

'You look great tonight anyway.' Now Clara was bracing. 'You'll knock him dead.'

She wished. Miriam turned and looked at herself in the mirror. Clara had come round as soon as she had got in from work, announcing she intended to keep her company until zero hour, as she'd put it.

Miriam had appreciated the thought, but in truth she'd rather have got ready in peace so she could go over—for the umpteenth time—the question-and-answer scenarios she'd played endlessly in her head since Tuesday. She felt so incredibly nervous, and now she was wondering if the plum jersey wool dress with a deep V-neck was dressy enough for dinner with Jay. She supposed it depended on where he was taking her, but Jay invariably favoured the more upmarket places.

She surveyed her reflection. Her black stiletto court shoes and ridiculously expensive designer jacket, which she had bought especially for tonight, gave the outfit that exclusive edge though, she comforted herself after another sweeping glance. They should do; they'd practically emptied her bank account.

'You'll be absolutely fine.' Clara had obviously read her thoughts. 'You will, Miriam. Really. Look, you're over him; that's what you have to keep telling yourself. You're the one in control now. OK?'

She could tell herself that all she wanted, but she knew the truth. Swallowing hard, Miriam muttered, 'What's the time?' just as the buzzer in the bedsit sounded. 'It's him.' Pure panic set in as she stared at Clara. 'I can't do this.'

'Of course you can.'

'I'm not like you.'

'That's true, you're not. No one's like me. At least, I hope not or else the effort I put in to being an original is totally wasted.' Clara gave another of her Cheshire-cat grins. 'Do you want me to answer?'

'No, I'll do it.' Taking a deep breath, Miriam pressed the button. 'Hello?'

'Miriam? It's Jay.'

Miriam's stomach did a somersault. 'I'll be right down.' There was no way she was going to give him the satisfaction of seeing how she lived now. The house she had rented with her friends when she'd met him hadn't exactly been the Ritz, but they'd had a lovely shared sitting room and kitchen-diner and each of their bedrooms had been a double. Not that she was ashamed of her bedsit, she told herself silently, but she wasn't going to give him any chance of crowing about her reduced circumstances.

'You'll be fine,' Clara said again after some moments when Miriam still hadn't moved. 'Here, take your bag.' She handed it to her, adding, 'Come on,' as she opened the bedsit door. 'I want to see him.'

'You can't.' Miriam stared at her in horror.

'I can. I'm going to get a paper at the shop down the road. Now, is it my fault your husband just happens to be standing on the doorstep when I open the door?'

'Clara, he'll know.'

'So?' Clara's voice was determined. 'Don't worry, he won't be in any doubt as to how I regard him, handsome or not.'

That was what worried her. Miriam followed Clara down the stairs as fast as her vertiginous heels would allow.

'Promise me you won't say anything,' she begged frantically. 'Promise me, Clara.'

'I promise.'

'Cross your heart and hope to die.'

'If you insist,' Clara said brightly over her shoulder.

'Say it.'

They had just reached the lobby and as Miriam clutched at Clara's arm the front door opened, the girl who shared Miriam's floor choosing that moment—of all moments—to make one of her rare trips home. Miriam wasn't really aware of Caroline's cheery 'Hi' as she sashayed past them, making for the stairs; her whole being was taken up with the tall, dark man who had put out a hand to prevent the door closing again.

'Hello, Miriam.'

She stared into the yellow-gold eyes that had fascinated her from day one. Everything about Jay had fascinated her, from his hard, handsome face with its thick eyelashes and sexy, slightly cynical mouth to his big muscled body that was as lean and toned as any prime athlete's. From somewhere she found the self-control to say fairly steadily, 'Hello, Jay.'

'I'm going to get a paper,' Clara announced to the lobby in general rather than anyone in particular, removing herself from Miriam's grip.

Miriam saw Jay's eyes widen as he took in the other girl, and he looked even more taken aback when Clara gave him a ferocious glare as she passed him without speaking. If she hadn't been feeling so wretched it would have made her smile, Miriam thought. As it was, she cleared her throat and said quietly, 'That was Clara. She lives here too.'

'Right.' His eyes had narrowed. 'I take it she knows about our current situation?'

'She's my friend.'

'So I gathered from the way she looked at me.' He waved his hand in the direction of the street. 'The taxi's waiting.'

He took her arm as she reached him and it took every ounce of Miriam's will for her not to reveal the trembling his touch caused.

He smelt as good as always. The thought was there at the back of her mind as they walked to the taxi-cab and Jay helped her inside with the natural courtesy that was an integral part of him. And he looked fantastic in a beautifully tailored suit and cream shirt and tie. But then he always looked fantastic, with or without clothes.

She turned her head to look out of the window as he sat down beside her, thankful he didn't have the power to read her wanton thoughts. And that last thought had started a process that was making her hot all over.

The taxi passed Clara, who had just reached the paper shop, and as Miriam saw the pink and mauve hair disappear into the confines of the building it was all she could do not to yell to the taxi driver to stop the car so she could dash in after her.

Jay had leaned back comfortably in the seat, his thigh touching hers and the big body relaxed. 'How are you?' he murmured as the tawny gaze glittered over her profile.

Miriam forced herself to glance briefly at him as she said, 'Very well. And you?'

'Oh, I'm great, Miriam. Just great. A different woman for every night of the week, of course; isn't that what you want to hear?' And then he said swiftly, 'Sorry, forget I said that. I attack when I'm nervous but then you know that.'

She had forgotten how seductive Jay's particular brand of ruthlessness married with vulnerability was. From their first date he had let his defences down when they were alone, something he didn't do with anyone else. At least, that was what she'd believed once. Along with the fact that he was a one-woman man.

Her thoughts made her voice tight when she said, 'I don't think this evening was a good idea, Jay. Whatever needs to be said could have been said over the phone.'

He made no comment to this, saying instead, 'You look beautiful tonight, but then you always do.'

Miriam knew she wasn't beautiful. She wouldn't break any mirrors but she had the sort of innocent, soft looks that maiden aunts called sweet and other women dismissed as no competition. Her mother's pet name for her as a child had been 'little dove', which said a lot really. What wasn't so obvious was that the temper that went with the red in her chestnut hair was there but hidden under layers of gentle friendliness. It rarely came into play but when it did it was fiery.

Aiming to keep the conversation as impersonal as possible, she said crisply, 'If you're wondering whether I intend to claim for anything, I'm not.'

Jay's eyes became gold slits. 'I'm sorry?'

'In the divorce settlement. I don't want anything. It's all yours anyway—the house, the cars, everything.'

There was a long pause. When Miriam nerved herself to look at him she saw his face was grim. 'Who's talking about divorce?'

'We are, surely.'

'You might be. I'm not.'

'But—'

'Have you instructed anyone at the practice?'

'Of course not. I'd discuss it with you first rather than

you just having the papers arrive in the post,' Miriam said with a touch of indignation in her voice.

'How thoughtful.' The sarcasm was biting.

Her soft mouth tightened. 'But it's clearly the next step.'

'It might be clear to you but that's as far as it goes, Miriam. For the record, when I stood at the altar I meant what I said. Till death and so on.'

If he carried on like this the death part might come quicker than he expected. Her anger rising, Miriam snapped, 'And I didn't? Is that what you're insinuating?'

'You're the one wanting a divorce.'

'And you're the one who slept with your secretary.'

Surprisingly, her lack of control seemed to restore his equilibrium. Leaning back in the seat again and slipping an arm along at the back of her, he said lazily, 'Don't shout, it makes you sound like a fishwife.'

Smouldering, she glared at him. 'I hate you.'

'Now you merely sound childish.'

Miriam had never been prone to any kind of physical violence but her fingers itched to wipe the mocking smile off his face. Instead she contented herself with moving as close to the edge of the seat as she could and keeping her eyes on the bright lights flashing by outside.

'Are you sulking?' Jay asked interestedly after a while.

'Isn't that what children do?' she bit back without looking at him, knowing her cheeks were burning and furious with herself for letting him get under her skin.

There was silence for a moment. 'You look lovely when you're angry,' he said, deadpan.

Suddenly—worryingly—she wanted to smile and she knew she couldn't. She was being subjected to the Carter charm and she knew from past history it was lethal. He could turn it on and off like a tap to get his own way. Forcing a calmness she didn't feel, Miriam said carefully, 'Jay, if this evening isn't going to be a complete disaster I suggest we keep things on a businesslike footing, OK?'

When she glanced at him there was a twist to the stern, sexy mouth that suggested he was amused. It ought to have made her more angry but it only served to remind her how much she still fancied him.

'You're my wife, Miriam. Not a business colleague.'

Fair comment—not that she'd acknowledge that. 'You know that's not the point,' she said evenly. 'We've been separated for ten months—'

'Not by my choice.'

She cleared her throat. 'Nevertheless, nothing's the same.'

'No, you're right; it isn't.'

Taken aback, she stared at him. She had expected him to argue, not agree with her. Ridiculously, it hurt. Recovering herself, she said weakly, 'There you are, then.'

'Where we *are* is the restaurant.' The cab drew up outside a brightly lit, glass-and-chrome type building as Jay spoke, the doorman standing outside and a glimpse of the swish interior convincing Miriam it was one of those places where the menu would be devoid of anything so crass as the price. 'I hope you're hungry. I've been here a couple of times since it opened in the summer and the food's great.'

Wondering who'd partnered him, Miriam said brightly, 'I'm starving,' knowing she'd have to force every morsel down over the lump in her throat. Over the last months she'd just about got the hang of training her mind to stop picturing Jay with other women but tonight it was beyond her.

Jay helped her out of the cab and paid the driver, taking

her elbow as he escorted her into the sumptuous confines of the restaurant. Immediately the maître d'hôtel was there, greeting Jay with a deferential warmth and leading them into a small lounge dotted with comfy leather sofas and low tables filled with nibbles as though they were royalty. Presenting them with two embossed menus which were works of art in themselves, he took their order for drinks and glided away.

Miriam looked down at her menu. It was in French and—thankfully—English. She'd been right, she thought dryly. There wasn't a price to be seen and the choice was staggering.

'See anything you fancy?' Jay drawled a minute or two later as though they were in some backstreet café. They both knew if anyone couldn't choose out of the incredible dishes on offer they didn't deserve to be sitting there.

Miriam didn't want to reveal how impressed she was. 'I think so,' she answered in like vein. 'I'll have the ginger-marinated salmon for starters and then tournedos of beef with wild mushrooms and orange-spiced armagnac plums.'

The wine waiter returned with their cocktails. Miriam had no idea what the sapphire martini she'd ordered would taste like but it had sounded elegant. She took a tentative sip. It was delicious. The Parfait d'Amour at the bottom of the glass was very blue and the slightly spicy Bombay Sapphire gin gave the cocktail a real kick. Warning herself it was probably very potent, she put the glass down. She needed to keep a clear head tonight; she *definitely* couldn't afford to be anything less than one hundred per cent compos mentis.

Jay surveyed her over his Manhattan. 'Not to your taste?'

'On the contrary,' she said politely, 'it's lovely.' She had forgotten what it was like to be with Jay, to be wined and dined and cosseted.

No, she hadn't, she corrected herself in the next breath. That was silly. Shutting out such memories had been part of the self-survival technique, that was all. She hadn't been able to afford to let the recollection of the good times— and there had been plenty—weaken her resolve.

Forcing her voice into neutral, Miriam tried not to let him see how he was affecting her. 'How's Jayne?'

'Is that a social nicety or are you really interested?'

That was unfair. Miriam's soft brown eyes darkened. From the day Jay had introduced her to his sister the two women had got on like a house on fire. Jay's parents had been killed ten years ago, when he was twenty-five and Jayne was sixteen. They'd been touring the States and had been involved in a freak accident when a car had left the road, mounted the pavement and killed them both instantly. Jayne had been staying with Jay while their parents were abroad and had continued to live with him until she had married a few months before Miriam and Jay had met.

'Don't look at me like that,' Jay said evenly. 'You've only made the effort to speak to her once or twice since we split up, so it's a fair question.'

'I didn't think it was fair to put Jayne in a position where she might have to take sides.' This was perfectly true. 'She thinks the world of you.'

'Meaning the side she would have taken would have been yours?'

Miriam wasn't going to be intimidated by the edge to his voice. 'I wasn't the one caught cavorting with someone else,' she pointed out coolly.

'Cavorting?' He seemed amused by her choice of word,

the dark expression on his face clearing. 'Miriam, puppies cavort. Or very young children.'

She saw nothing funny in this. 'I obviously have a different slant on adultery from you.'

'You're still set on believing what you want to believe.'

'Want to believe?' Coolness went out of the window. 'Don't you try and turn this round on me, Jay.'

The immaculate waiter who was to take their order appeared at the table and Miriam curbed her frustration. Dredging up a smile, she gave her choice of dishes and Jay followed with his. Once they were alone again, he said quietly, 'Jayne's just had it confirmed she's pregnant, as it happens. They're over the moon.'

'That's wonderful.' Briefly their differences were forgotten. 'I'm so pleased for her.'

'Will you call her and tell her that yourself?'

Their eyes met and held. 'I—I don't want to upset her.'

'You won't,' Jay said firmly.

Panic gripped her, squeezing her voice box so her words emerged tight and high when she said, 'Jay, there has to be a cut-off point, you know that as well as I do. Neither of us needs complications…' That hadn't sounded right. 'I don't want to cause difficulties in your family.'

'You're my family, Miriam. Haven't you realised that yet? Damn it, no one else—not even Jayne—impinges on us.'

For a second she drowned in the golden sea of his eyes, letting his words wash over her. She wanted to believe him more than anything else in the world, but she couldn't.

Icy cold reality crashed in a wave over her head. 'Jay, it's over.'

'Never in a hundred years.' He leaned forward, his body warmth enveloping her as she sat rigid and still. 'You're my wife; I've never felt about any woman the way I feel about you.'

'It's a pity you didn't think about that before you got involved with Belinda.'

For a long moment his eyes assessed her, then she saw him breathe out slowly. 'For such a soft, gentle little thing you've got a will of iron, haven't you?' he murmured wryly. 'But you won't win this one, Miriam. And do you know why? Because, at the very bottom of you, you don't want to win. You know as well as I do that we were meant to be together.'

She looked into the hard, handsome face. He was deadly serious. The strong planes of his jaw, the determined thrust to his chin were evidence that he meant every word. Almost imperceptibly, she held herself straighter. 'Don't tell me what I want and don't want,' she said very clearly.

She saw the flash of surprise in his eyes. 'Can you deny it?'

She wanted to shout at him, to pour all the hurt and anger and betrayal over his head in a bitter, acidic flood of hate, but that would be playing straight into his hands. She wouldn't let him see how she was hurting; she'd rather walk on hot coals. And she wouldn't make a scene, much as she would have loved to throw the rest of her cocktail into his face and march out of the restaurant.

Miriam took a deep breath. 'I want a divorce,' she said expressionlessly. 'That's the only reason I've come here tonight. You can believe me or choose to think there's still something between us—it doesn't matter in the long run.'

The words hung between them before falling like pieces of ice, the muted chatter from the other tables and soft music that was playing on the perimeter of their world for two.

'You've changed.' It wasn't laudatory.

'Yes, I have.' She marvelled at the calmness of her voice, considering how she was trembling inside. 'I'm no longer the foolish young woman who married you. Who believed you when you said we'd grow old together, have children, grandchildren…'

'You were never foolish, Miriam,' he said quietly. 'Wary, unsure—just how unsure I've only come to appreciate in the last months. I thought when I gave you the space you said you needed you'd work things out for yourself but I hadn't bargained for how deep the hurt over your father had gone. You don't trust men, do you? Any men. Not even me.'

Especially not you. Her chin rose. 'In other words our separation is all my fault? You're whiter than white, I suppose?'

'I've never been whiter than white.' He smiled rue-fully.

Miriam stared at him, wondering how he could smile when her body was so tense it hurt. *I can't deal with this*, she thought suddenly. *I need to leave. I have to get out before I make a fool of myself.*

As the thought hit the waiter reappeared like a genie out of a bottle. 'If you would care to follow me, your table is ready,' he said smoothly, whisking their half-finished drinks onto the small round tray he was carrying and then preceding them out of the lounge and into the main restaurant.

Miriam had no choice but to follow as Jay stood to his feet and took her arm. She glanced at him, trying to read his expression, but his face was wearing the cool, remote mask he could adopt at will. He obviously didn't want her to know what he was feeling.

Once seated at a table for two, Miriam glanced round the glittering room. It was elegant and chic, the quiet hum of conversation from the assembled diners and the light, easy music from the quartet in a corner of the restaurant making a pleasant background to a meal.

Jay's eyes were tight on her when her gaze came to rest on him. 'I've missed evenings with you like this,' he murmured softly. 'Along with evenings at home, of course, Sunday mornings in bed with the papers, waking up together, walks on the heath—'

'Don't, Jay.'

'Why?' He swallowed the last of his cocktail. 'It's the truth, and if I can't say it to my wife, who can I say it to?'

'Your current girlfriend?' Miriam suggested, as much to see his reaction as anything else.

'I don't have a girlfriend, Miriam.' Jay's smile said he knew what she was about. 'I'm married, remember?'

'It's not me who has forgotten that.'

The wine waiter appeared with the bottle Jay had ordered for the table. After Jay had given his approval to what turned out to be a richly flavoured red, the waiter poured a little wine into each of their glasses and then glided away.

Miriam had used the time to remind herself that she couldn't afford to let Jay see he could get under her skin. She had to remain aloof and composed; it was her only armour against his quick mind and charm.

'Relax, Miriam.'

His next words tested her resolve. Flushing, she forced herself to speak calmly when she said, 'I am relaxed.'

Before she was aware of it he had reached across the table and taken her cold hand in his, so close she could scent his male warmth. Straightening her fingers, which she only now realised had been clenched tight, he gently stroked her flesh. Tingles shot up her arm but she willed herself to remain perfectly still as he whispered, 'Such soft, silky skin.'

She wanted to tell him that he didn't have the right to touch her whenever he liked, not any more. He had relinquished that last Christmas, but although the words were there she couldn't get them past the lump in her dry throat.

The tawny-gold eyes continued to search her face as the silence grew. Somehow Miriam managed to break their hold and turn her face away but Jay wouldn't let her fingers go so easily. She still didn't say anything, basically because she couldn't. His touch was invoking so many memories, memories she had locked away and kept buried for ten long months.

'Talk to me,' he murmured huskily. 'We have to talk, you must see that? We used to be able to say anything to each other.'

She almost lost control at that moment. Pain and anger swept through her in equal measure and if they had been anywhere else she would have let them have free rein. How dared he remind her of how they had been, she thought with blind agony. When they had lived together they'd shared every thought, every problem, sometimes talking half the night away. He had been her rock, her fortress, and she supposed she had set him on some sort of pedestal in her heart, which had made it all the harder when she had had to face the fact that her idol had feet of clay.

Easing the air past the constriction in her throat, she pulled her hand away. She was trembling and she prayed he couldn't see it. 'I don't know what you want from me, Jay, but whatever it is, it's no good. When I said it was over I meant it.'

'I don't believe that.' He leaned back in his seat once

more but didn't take his gaze from her face. 'I will never believe it.'

'Whether you believe it or not doesn't really matter.' Her voice was calm but part of her was dying inside. It felt as though the pain and trauma of the night she'd seen him with Belinda was just as acute.

She had been crazy to agree to see him like this, she told herself feverishly. She should have let the legal system take charge. She knew from her experiences through her work that once the machine began grinding little could stop it. Sentiment and emotion became lost under mountains of paperwork and the phrases the solicitors and legal experts did so well. Cold, clinical words that dissected and separated two lives with the minimum of feeling and fuss.

'You're serious, aren't you?' There was a touch of incredulity in his voice now. 'You're actually going to let that spiteful woman accomplish what she intended. Can't you see she wanted to come between us all along?'

'Of course I see that,' she bit back; she'd never imagined anything else. Just because Belinda had set her sights on him that didn't excuse what he'd done, though.

'And you're going to let her win?'

'This is not a game, Jay.'

'You're damn right it's not.' His voice was not loud but edged with fury.

'I'm glad we agree on something.' Her words were clipped, tight.

For a moment she thought he was going to stand up and grab her and march out of the restaurant, but as she watched she saw him breathe in and out and take control of the anger that had etched itself into the handsome features. Slowly the mask settled into place. It was an abject lesson on the amazing will of the man.

When he next spoke his voice was low and quiet. 'I love you. Do you still love me?'

Her eyes enormous, she stared at him. It was the last thing she had expected him to say.

'Do you, Miriam?'

For the first time since she had met him Miriam realised what had made him so powerful and formidable in business. She knew he had a reputation for ruthlessness but he had never been that way with her, not for a moment. But now the big-cat eyes were unblinking and predatory as they scoured her white face, looking for a chink in her armour, for any sign of weakness. Somehow she managed to lie. 'No,' she said.

Even to herself she didn't sound very convincing.

His expression remained impassive but she thought she saw something in his eyes, a glimmer of reaction, but she couldn't be sure. Nervously she reached for her cocktail and finished it to give her hands something to do, glancing across the beautiful room and wondering if anyone else felt as wretched as she did.

'I'll give you your divorce—I'll even make it nice and easy for you—on one condition,' Jay said silkily after a tense few moments had ticked by.

Feeling as though she had been hit by a sledgehammer, which was totally illogical as she was the one demanding a divorce, Miriam stuttered, 'W-what condition?'

'That you convince me it's what you really want.'

'I've told you,' she managed to say more steadily.

'That doesn't do it.'

Miriam frowned. 'If you don't believe me when I say

it, how can I convince you?' Immediately she'd said it she knew she had played straight into his hands.

His firm, sexy mouth mocked her with its wryness. 'Come back to the apartment and live with me again for the few weeks till Christmas,' he said easily, as though he wasn't asking the impossible. 'See how you feel then.'

Her absolute amazement changed to outrage. 'I can't believe you just said that.'

'Not as man and wife if you don't want to share my bed,' he said calmly. 'You can have the spare room if that makes you feel better.'

'It wouldn't.' Dark eyebrows rose, and in answer to the glitter in his eyes she said quickly, 'What I mean is, I've no intention of coming back to the apartment whether I could stay in the spare room or not. And I would stay in it, of course, if I was coming back.'

'Which you're not,' he put in helpfully.

'No, I'm not.' Suddenly she realised she hated that apartment. It had always been Jay's, never hers. She had never felt at home there, more like a visitor who was being tolerated by the masculine surroundings and ultra-modern gadgets. Other girlfriends had been there, of course, she knew that. She had never had the nerve to ask him if they had slept in his bed but they must have done.

'What's the matter? What are you thinking now?'

She hadn't been aware that her thoughts had mirrored themselves in the painful twist to her mouth and the darkening of her soft brown eyes, but as always Jay saw too much. Swiftly she wiped her face clear of expression. 'Nothing.'

'Nothing didn't put that look on your face,' Jay said grimly. 'Tell me.'

What the hell! He'd asked for it. 'I never want to step

foot in the apartment again, if you want to know,' she said with a flatness that said far more than a raised voice could have done. 'It was never a home to me and it was always yours, never mine. I was merely a guest there.'

Now it was his turn to be amazed. 'You never said.'

Miriam shrugged. 'It was your home and you loved it. The first time you showed me round I could see how much it meant to you. Besides which—'

'What?'

'I didn't realise quite how much it would remain yours,' she said, a trifle illogically.

He seemed to understand, though. 'And how much did it?'

'A hundred per cent.'

'I see.'

'Oh, it's stunning,' she said quickly, wondering why she was trying to sweeten the pill after what he'd done. 'Absolutely fabulous and I can understand why you love it, of course, but it's not...me.'

Jay's jaw tightened. 'But you didn't think to tell me you hated it.'

'I didn't hate it—' Miriam stopped abruptly. Why was she lying to make him feel better? 'Actually I did,' she said as much to herself as Jay. 'Especially when we gave dinner parties and things like that. I always felt as though I was one of those hostesses who are hired for the evening.'

Jay looked appalled. 'I had no idea you were so unhappy,' he said stiffly.

'Nor had I.' That sounded ridiculous. 'What I mean is, I wasn't unhappy exactly, not with us, but—' Miriam shrugged again '—I did all the fitting in.'

'Most women would give their eye-teeth to live over-looking the river.'

She'd really offended him. Miriam found she didn't care and was faintly horrified by it. Perhaps it was the 'most women' bit that had caught her on the raw. Sweetly, she said, 'I'm not most women, Jay. I'm me.'

Jay, through slightly gritted teeth, said, 'That you are.'

'Ginger-marinated salmon?' The waiter was at their sides with their first course.

'That's me,' said Miriam. Again.

Their plates having been deposited in front of them with a flourish and offers of extra sauces refused, the waiter disappeared with a polite, 'Enjoy your meal.'

Jay had chosen hot-smoked trout and chive tartlet but he was staring at it ferociously. Raising his eyes to hers, he growled, 'I can't believe you felt that way and didn't tell me. How can you blame me for something I was unaware of?'

'I didn't blame you.' It was true; she hadn't. Not at the time anyway. It was only after Belinda it had really begun to rankle. 'I'd probably have never mentioned it if you hadn't suggested me coming back to live in the apartment.'

If it was possible his face darkened still more. 'That makes it worse, not better. What else are you holding against me, for crying out loud?'

'Now you're being unreasonable.'

'Me?' He took several long gulps of wine as though he needed it. 'You sit there and tell me you hated every minute in our home, something you hid pretty successfully while you lived there, I might add, and you object because I ask you what else you didn't like? It's a pretty fair question from where I'm standing.'

He was sitting, but Miriam didn't feel it was the time to point that out.

'I'm beginning to feel I never knew you,' he said darkly after a moment or two.

It hurt. Determined not to let him see, Miriam stared at him steadily. 'Then you're experiencing a little of what I've felt since Christmas.'

He swore, softly and under his breath, but it was so unlike him Miriam knew he was really angry. Still, that was all to the good, wasn't it? she asked herself silently. He would be more likely to accept her decision that she wanted a divorce if he didn't want her any more.

Miserably she picked up her knife and fork and began to eat. If she had needed any further convincing that their marriage was well and truly over, tonight had provided it.

CHAPTER THREE

'So…' Their empty plates had been whisked away some moments before and Jay was surveying her thoughtfully. 'If you don't want to come and live in the apartment, how about I join you in the bedsit?'

For a second Miriam thought he was joking. Then she looked full into the hard, handsome face and saw he wasn't. 'That's impossible,' she said firmly, colour flooding her face. The thought of the two of them in her tiny home—not to mention her sofa bed—was too intimate for words.

'Why?'

'It's only big enough for one—they all are.' Then she realised she was actually giving credence to his crazy suggestion by her answer. 'But that's beside the point,' she added quickly. 'I want a divorce, Jay. Not to live with you again.'

'I know that.' He took a long swallow of wine, watching her for a moment. 'But I can make a divorce easy or difficult, and when I say difficult, I mean difficult. You know me, Miriam. I don't make idle threats.' The yellow-gold eyes had hardened, his mouth set uncompromisingly.

It would be emotional suicide to live with him again; she knew that with every fibre of her being. However difficult he made things, she couldn't do it.

Whether Jay read her thoughts she didn't know, but the next moment he drained his glass, pouring himself another before he drawled, 'OK, how about we meet halfway? You live in your place and I'll live in mine—' he caught himself, smiling wryly as he corrected '—ours, but we see each other in our spare time.'

Miriam thought this must be the weirdest conversation ever between two people in their situation. Although perhaps not, she realised in the next instant. There had been a case at work between a married couple who were divorcing but had agreed to share their house along with their new respective partners and six children. The whole lot had lived together in practically a commune set-up, with even one of the mother-in-laws squeezed into the house somewhere and two dogs and three cats.

Oh, what was she thinking of the McBrides for right now? she asked herself impatiently. Shock, most likely. Her mind was retreating because it couldn't believe what it was being asked to consider. Pulling herself together, she tried to sound stern and assertive. 'You know as well as I do that that's ridiculous.'

'Impossible, ridiculous… When did you become so negative, Miriam?' Jay drawled mildly.

'It's not being negative, it's plain common sense.'

'You mean like wearing a vest in winter and eating up all your greens and being in bed by ten every night?'

'No.' Her soft voice sharpened. He was making her out to be as dull as ditch water. 'There's just no point to it; anyone can see that.'

'I'm anyone and I can't.'

Jay Carter wasn't anyone, Miriam thought faintly. Whatever he was, and her opinion on that changed countless times a day, he most definitely was not just anyone. Her freckles were threatening to explode off her pink face as she said, 'Jay, why are you doing this?'

'I've told you. I don't want a divorce. I've never taken the easy way out of anything and I don't intend to start now. I can see there are cracks wide enough to drive a car down in what I thought was a perfect marriage, not least the fact my wife hates my guts and our home and probably everything else we had together, but I'm not prepared to wind things up without at least attempting to try and iron out the problems.' He had leaned back in his chair as he'd been speaking, the lights overhead turning his black hair ebony-blue and his chiselled features as classically pure as a work of art.

As Miriam gazed at him the old feeling that had been with her almost from the first time they'd met and which had never completely gone away, not even after they were married, returned in a flood. How could a man who looked like Jay did, a man who had everything—wit, personality, wealth and a body to die for—want her? One of her friends, in the aftermath of the separation, had voiced what Miriam knew lots of people were thinking. She hadn't meant to be anything other than helpful but her words had confirmed more than anything else how folk saw her and Jay. Angela had taken her hand and said softly, 'Miriam, look at it this way: Jay's…extraordinary, and if he comes home to you each night, does it really matter if he strays now and again? A man like him, well, you've got to expect it, haven't you? And he did marry you.'

Meaning, what else could you ask for? Miriam thought now. An ordinary, unremarkable girl bagging the sort of guy who only comes along once in a blue moon, she ought to be down on her knees thanking God he'd looked her way.

'Well?' Jay's voice was lazy and relaxed but the amber eyes were piercingly intent. 'Decision time. On the one hand we date for a little while and see how things sort out, on the other I make your life…uncomfortable.'

'You'd do that?' she asked, white-faced.

'In these circumstances? Yes, I would,' he replied without a shred of remorse.

'How can you say you love me and behave like that?'

'It's because I love you I'd behave like that, Miriam.'

'I don't see love the way you do obviously.'

'Considering this is from the woman who clearly kept more from me than she told me and who didn't care enough for me to stay and talk things out, not to mention trust me, forgive me if I'm not too perturbed by that,' he murmured, one eyebrow slanting mockingly.

Miriam glared at him. How dared he criticise her and act holier-than-thou? Out of marks of ten for sheer nerve, Jay scored twenty. 'If you're that concerned about us, why didn't you make more effort to see me months ago?' she said from the heart, regretting it the moment the words were out.

'Because it wasn't working, me trying to put things right,' he answered immediately, his cool tone belying the glitter of anger in his eyes her words had caused. 'You weren't prepared to listen and I was blowed if I was going to keep on banging my head against a brick wall.'

'So what's changed?' she said icily.

Before she could stop him he had leant forward and taken her small, slender hand in his, lacing her fingers through his and holding them tight. 'I realised one person in this relationship has to start behaving like a grown-up, and it sure as hell isn't going to be you, my love,' he said softly. 'That and the fact that you want me.'

She wanted to tell him that she most certainly did not want him. That he was the last man on earth she wanted, in fact. That she'd rather walk through London stark naked than have anything to do with him in the future. She wanted to, but her mouth failed to form the words. All she could manage was a somewhat feeble, 'Huh.'

'When you look at me you look at me with hungry eyes, Miriam. You remember what it was like, don't you...?' He let the words trickle like warm honey over her taut nerves. 'The things we did, the way I made you feel. I was your first lover and I did more than have sex with you, I *loved* you, but you only opened your body to me. Your mind, that inner self, you gave me no access to. I gave you your first taste of sexual ecstasy, your first climax, but I fooled myself when I thought I had you. I shan't make that mistake again.'

He turned her hand over in his, bending his head and caressing the wildly beating pulse in her wrist with his warm lips.

Miriam shivered, she couldn't help it. His touch had always invoked a tumult of feeling in every nerve and sinew and she was as helpless before it now as she had been in the very beginning.

He raised his head, the tawny gaze watching the effect he had on her. 'You see?' he said softly. 'You can't escape the truth—you're part of me. We're husband and wife.'

'Not any more.' She wanted to snatch her hand away but was aware she couldn't cause a scene. 'Only on paper.'

'What we have doesn't begin or end with a piece of paper. You're mine, Miriam. You'll always be mine, but I realise now it's not enough that you're my wife. I want to know you inside out; how you think and feel and why you're like you are. I haven't even begun to touch the inner core, have I? That private self that trusts and believes in the beloved.'

Finally she managed to retrieve her hand and with some distance between them she found she could think again. 'We're in the position we're in because you had an affair with your secretary,' she said flatly.

Jay expelled a quiet breath. 'No I didn't,' he said very quietly, 'but that's nothing to do with the position we're in. Sooner or later we would have been here; it was just a fact waiting to happen. At some point you would have convinced yourself I was like your father because you weren't prepared to let yourself believe anything else. If you did it might make you vulnerable.'

'That's rubbish.' She lifted her chin in angry defiance, prepared to fight tooth and nail for what she saw as her integrity.

'I don't think so. And everything you've said tonight confirms it. It would have been the most natural thing in the world for you to tell me you didn't want to live in the apartment, so why didn't you? I'll tell you why. Because you didn't want to risk displeasing me. You told me your mother lived like that with your father, falling in with everything he wanted in order to keep his love.'

'That's not why I didn't tell you.'

He refused to accept her self-denial. 'Think about it, Miriam. Tonight, when you're alone. Think about what I've said because sooner or later you've got to start facing your gremlins.'

He glanced over her shoulder as she glared at him, his voice suddenly casual as he murmured, 'Here's our main course. Smile, Miriam. You don't want to frighten the nice waiter, now, do you?'

She waited until the waiter had left again before she said, 'Anyone else in your position would do the decent thing.'

'Really?' Jay smiled but it didn't reach his eyes. 'And what's that?'

'Make the divorce as painless as possible.'

'Not even an option,' he said cheerfully. 'My meal's great by the way. How's yours?'

'Jay—'

'Eat your dinner.' Suddenly all amusement was gone and the tender note to his voice was nearly her undoing. 'We're not going to talk about this any more tonight, we're going to enjoy ourselves. Perhaps even dance in a while, OK?'

Not OK. So not OK. 'I don't think—'

'Good. I don't want you to think. Just to feel.'

If he interrupted her a third time he'd *feel* her foot making contact with his shin bone. Miriam became aware the couple at the next table were looking at them with thinly veiled curiosity. They were not near enough to have heard the content of their conversation but she didn't doubt her body language had said quite enough for them to get the message all was not well. Taking a long silent breath, she glanced down at her plate. The beef looked wonderful and perhaps because she'd hardly eaten anything the last couple of days, worrying about tonight, she suddenly found her mouth was watering. Picking up her knife and fork, she began to eat.

CHAPTER FOUR

'So you're telling me that, after all the talk about wanting you back and living together and everything, he didn't even ask for a goodnight kiss?'

Clara was sitting cross-legged on Miriam's sofa eating a croissant, the crumbs of which were scattering in an arc about her. Miriam had long since got used to her friend's aversion for sitting at a table; in Clara's bedsit meals were either eaten balanced precariously on two long-legged stools at the tiny breakfast bar, or sitting hippy-fashion on one of several massive floor cushions. She had also got used to her friend's tactlessness. Nodding now, she said flatly, 'After all that was said he was probably glad to see the back of me. Anyway, I wouldn't have kissed him if he'd wanted me to, you know that.'

Clara didn't comment on this questionable statement. Instead she licked her fingers one by one and then said in a wise-owl tone, 'He's playing it cool.'

If he was playing it cool it was arctic-cold, Miriam thought miserably. After their initial talk at dinner Jay had suddenly switched to suave and amusing dinner-companion mode, steering the conversation away from anything personal when she had attempted to get down to the nitty-gritty of their separation and refusing to be drawn when she'd sensed what he was doing. He had been witty and charming and polite, as though it were the first time they'd dated, and when he'd seen her home in the taxi he'd made no attempt to kiss her or even hold her hand. And it had driven her mad; she'd tossed and turned all night wondering why he'd changed his mind about wanting her.

And how was that for inconsistency on her part? she asked herself as Clara helped herself to another croissant. Clara had arrived on her doorstep at eight o'clock positively agog to hear how the evening had gone, and she hadn't had the heart to send her away, even though she'd only finally gone to sleep as dawn had broken.

Miriam watched her friend tuck into the pastry and found herself envying Clara's happy-go-lucky approach to life and love more than she'd ever done before. She wished with all her heart she had just a smidgen of Clara's carefree, permissive attitude. With this in mind, and also to deflect any more humiliating disclosures, she said brightly, 'How's Dave?'

'Who?' said Clara, without any attempt at joking. 'Oh, Dave.'

'History?' Miriam guessed, feeling a bit sorry for the hapless Dave. He had had a great taste in wine.

Clara nodded. 'I've actually decided to be celibate for a while,' she said, reaching for her third croissant. 'There's a guy at work I've been talking to and he's been celibate for over a year now. He reckons his work output has increased by a hundred per cent and he feels terrific. In tune with himself. You know?'

Miriam didn't. She'd never felt in tune with herself in the whole of her life. Which perhaps meant Jay had got a point. This was too disturbing to contemplate and she said brightly, 'Another coffee?'

'Love one.' Clara fixed her with her great blue eyes, which were outlined in a murky, yellow gold that morning. It should have looked gross but on Clara it simply looked right. 'So, are you seeing Jay again, then? Date-wise, I mean?' she asked, uncurling herself off the sofa and wandering across to the window.

Miriam made an indeterminate sound that could have meant anything and shrugged. 'I don't think so. There's no point, is there?' Not for the world would she admit, not even to Clara, that he had said goodnight and walked away without mentioning seeing her again.

Not that she wanted him to, she hastened to assure herself. Of course not. She would have to say no and things would get awkward again and the whole uncomfortable cycle would start once more. Far better they parted civilly, having shared a nice meal. It was just that she didn't appreciate him blowing hot and cold the way he had last night, one minute saying he wanted them to make a go of it and live together again, and the next dumping her on her doorstep without so much as a by-your-leave.

Handing Clara her coffee, she said, 'We'll have to go shopping for ski clothes soon. We can't leave it till the last minute.'

With typical directness Clara ignored Miriam's attempt to change the subject. 'He's got under your skin again, hasn't he? I knew it was a bad idea, you going last night.'

'He hasn't.' She'd spoken too quickly. After a charged silence in which Clara's pierced eyebrows rose, Miriam repeated weakly, 'He hasn't. It was just a big unsettling, that's all. We were—are—married, Clara.'

'But you're over him.'

'Definitely.'

'It wouldn't worry you, then, that he's just got out of a sex machine on wheels and is about to ring the doorbell?'

'You're joking!' Miriam flew across to the window. Clara wasn't joking. Miriam just had time to see Jay raise his hand before the intercom's buzz sounded. 'I can't see him.' She stared aghast at Clara. She was still in her pyjamas and she hadn't even brushed her hair, she thought wildly.

'Don't worry, I'll get rid of him.' Clara marched over to the intercom and pressed the button. 'Hello?'

'Miriam?' Deep and resonant, Jay's voice cut into the room.

'No, this is Clara, Miriam's friend. She's not here.'

There was silence for a moment. 'Why are you there if she isn't?' he asked suspiciously.

'I like her bedsit better than mine. It's tidier.'

True, Miriam thought. Ridiculous answer, but true none the less.

'Put Miriam on, would you?' Jay's voice had an edge to it.

'Can't, sorry. I told you, she's not here,' Clara lied merrily, clearly enjoying herself.

'It's eight-thirty on a Saturday morning. Where the hell is she if she's not at home?' Jay grated, losing patience.

'Work?' Clara suggested sweetly.

'She doesn't work on a Saturday.'

'Shopping?'

There was a pregnant pause. 'Now, look here—'

Pushing Clara aside, Miriam said quietly, 'Hello, Jay. What can I do for you?'

There was another pause, longer this time. Miriam could

hear her heart beating, the blood thundering in her ears. She found she was holding her breath and forced herself to breathe out slowly, aware of Clara's eyes on her.

'I need to talk to you,' he said with dangerous softness after some moments.

With Clara waving her arms and mouthing 'No!', Miriam found her thought process had frozen. 'Why?' she murmured stupidly.

'I'd prefer to discuss that face-to-face.'

'I'm still in my pyjamas.'

This time his voice had a smoky quality to it when he said, 'I've seen you in pyjamas before. And without them.'

Miriam was not about to go there. Especially with Clara's eagle eyes on her. Refusing to blush, she said crisply, 'Give me a couple of minutes to get changed and then come up,' as she pressed the release for the door.

'I knew it,' Clara said with infuriating smugness. 'He's worked the old magic, hasn't he?'

Now colour did creep up into Miriam's cheeks. 'Clara, I have to change. You don't mind cutting breakfast short?'

'I do, but not because of the food. I don't want your heart broken again.'

There was real concern in Clara's voice and spontaneously Miriam hugged her, nearly impaling her forehead on the spiky hair, which was lacquered as stiff as a board this morning. 'I'll be fine. Don't worry. One thing I'm absolutely sure about is that Jay and I are finished. I couldn't go back there, Clara. I know that. But if we can agree to do this in a relatively friendly fashion it'll make things so much easier. Believe me, I know how it can be when the two parties are fighting and it isn't pretty. I see it every day at work.'

Clara looked at her. 'You're too nice for him,' she said

feelingly. 'I'd want my pound of flesh if I were in your position.' Tilting her head, she added, 'Actually you're probably too nice to be friends with me but I'm glad you are.' Hugging Miriam back, she then made her way to the door. 'I'll talk to him for five minutes to give you time to titivate.'

'No, Clara, don't.'

Her words fell on deaf ears. Clara had already shut the door behind her. Miriam groaned. Great. If she'd wanted the final straw in this little scenario Clara had just provided a cartload.

Whisking off her pyjamas, she grabbed a vest top and combat trousers from her wardrobe—her usual Saturday cleaning-the-bedsit-and-messing-about clothes, and she was blowed if she was going to change the routine and dress up for Jay—and ran a comb through her thick hair. She couldn't resist glancing in the mirror. Without any make-up her freckles dominated her creamy skin and made her look about sixteen, and her slim figure and wide, guileless eyes completed the picture of naivety. She clicked her tongue in annoyance. She was as far removed from the elegant, so-phisticated beauties who populated Jay's world as the man in the moon, and about as seductive, she told herself ir-ritably. She had nothing about her to entice a male and drive him crazy—she didn't even have Clara's individuality.

She pushed back a strand of chestnut hair from one flushed cheek, searching her reflection for what had at-tracted Jay in the first place. After a few moments she admitted defeat. It was as big a mystery to her now as it had been when they'd met, she thought, turning away, but then stopping in her tracks.

Jay had accused her last night of never trusting him, of biding time until he betrayed her as her father had betrayed her mother. *Had* she felt like that? She hadn't thought she had. She had loved him beyond life.

But love wasn't trust. A separate part of her mind was playing devil's advocate. You could love someone without trusting them—she only had to look at her mother with her father to know that was true. Shortly after her mother had got together with George, she'd confided to Miriam that this relationship was as different from the one she'd had with Miriam's father as chalk from cheese. 'Until I met George I'd never realised I hadn't trusted your father from even before our marriage,' Anne had murmured quietly. 'Your father was so handsome and charismatic, I suppose. He drew people to him like moths to a flame, especially the women,' she had added without any bitterness at all. 'They threw themselves at him. He was just one of those men; it wasn't his fault.'

Had she been waiting for history to repeat itself? Miriam asked herself sickly. No; no, she hadn't. She was sure she hadn't. Jay was twisting things, that was all. But the thought still niggled as she went to the door, opening it and intending to call down the stairs for Jay to come up.

But he wasn't downstairs with Clara. He was leaning against the wall opposite the door, his hands in his trouser pockets and his tawny eyes narrowed. His big black leather jacket and black jeans made his flagrant masculinity even more threatening than usual and her heart flipped at the sight of him. 'I—I thought you were talking to Clara,' she said inanely, taken off her guard.

'The pit bull?' he murmured pleasantly. 'I saw no point in prolonging a conversation with her when she clearly wanted to rip my throat out.'

'Clara's a very good friend,' Miriam said defensively.

'I'm sure people said that about Attila the Hun and Ivan the Terrible but I wouldn't have been interested in getting to know them either.' His eyes narrowed still more. 'Aren't you going to invite me in?'

'Of course.' She stood aside for him to enter as though she didn't hate the fact he was invading her private domain, closing the door and watching him as he glanced round the high-ceilinged room.

'Cosy.'

It could have been patronising but even though she wanted to find fault with him Miriam knew he was being genuine. 'I think so,' she said quietly.

'A little nest with a bird's-eye view,' he added, strolling over to the window and gazing out over the vista of rooftops and buildings touched with the morning sunshine. 'How often do you sit and lose yourself in that expanse of sky?'

He knew her too well. Crisply, she said, 'When time permits.'

He turned, shrugging off his leather jacket and throwing it over the back of the sofa. 'I can smell coffee,' he hinted, glancing at the remaining croissants. 'Are those going begging?'

She could do nothing else but invite him to sit down, which he did with alacrity. Miriam busied herself fixing some fresh coffee and putting out more preserves to go with the croissants, trying not to think about how good he looked. He was wearing a pale lilac shirt tucked into his jeans, open-necked and with the sleeves partly rolled up. Narrow-waisted and lean-hipped, with broad shoulders, he looked like every young maiden's dream—probably their mother's dream too, she thought wryly. She could remember too many occasions when every woman in the room had been fluttering around his orbit. Thinking about it now, there had been too many dinner parties, too many functions and social gatherings where she'd had to smile and chat and pretend she didn't notice some female or other turning inside out to get Jay's attention.

'I hope I didn't interrupt your breakfast with the pit bull,' Jay said mildly as she placed the fresh pot of coffee on the small bistro table before sitting down on the other chair.

'Her name is Clara.' She fixed him with stern eyes. 'And like I said, she's a good friend.'

'I'm glad,' he said softly, all amusement gone. 'I didn't like to think of you existing with strangers.'

It was expedient to ignore the note in his voice; she didn't like what the tender quality did to her resolve to stay distant and aloof. Pouring them both a cup of coffee, she said flatly, 'What is it you need to talk to me about?' as she handed Jay's to him.

'Us.'

Her cup rattled on her saucer and she quickly put it down. 'I thought we did that last night.'

'We did. In part. But Rome wasn't built in a day.'

'Meaning?'

'I've finally got it through my obviously thick skull that what I thought was a great marriage wasn't,' Jay said very calmly. 'You're a bundle of contradictions and secrets, Miriam, but I'm willing to persevere with you.'

'Thank you so much,' she bit back sarcastically.

'It's a pleasure.' He grinned unrepentantly. 'The rewards will be worth it in the end.' He'd devoured two croissants; now he reached for a third. 'I think I'll call in for breakfast more often, by the way—these are superb.'

'Jay, we're getting a divorce. That doesn't usually mean

a couple breakfast together,' she said more calmly than she was feeling.

One eyebrow slanted provocatively. 'No? Perhaps they should. Anyway, who says we're getting a divorce?'

Miriam chose her words carefully. 'I don't want us to be enemies any more than you do, but I'm serious about this, Jay.'

'And you think I'm not?' The tawny eyes took on the texture of hard amber. 'Then you know me as little as I apparently knew you.'

She stared at him. She would never win in a war of words—his mind was too quick, too agile, too altogether intimidating for any opponent who was foolish enough to take Jay Carter on. Without knowing it, she used a weapon that sliced through his composure like a knife through butter. Quietly, she said, 'I don't know what to say to you. I only know how I feel. I can't be your wife any more and survive, Jay.' Her words rang with honesty. 'If anything remains of the love you said you felt for me, you'll let me go.'

He stood up, a muscle clenching in his square jaw and his voice as low as hers had been when he said, 'If anything remains? Hell, Miriam, you've really got no idea, have you? Can't you just for one minute stop thinking of yourself as the betrayed victim and allow yourself to imagine what I might be feeling? My only crime is loving you. That's it. And for that I've been hung, drawn and quartered.'

'Don't—don't do this.'

'What? Love you?' He pulled her up and into his arms, kissing her hard.

She knew she ought to object, to fight him, to pull away. She knew it in her head but her heart and body were saying something else. She'd missed him so much—for ten long months she had tried to pretend she hated him, but all along she'd known she was fooling herself. Jay was the only man she had ever loved and would ever love. She didn't want it to be that way—in fact, she would give everything she possessed for it to be different—but that was the way she was made. A one-man woman. And the man was Jay.

'I—I can't...'

He kissed the words from her lips, his tongue rippling along her teeth and then taking the sweetness of her mouth. Almost immediately the kiss changed in tempo, his mouth moving with more pressure over hers, parting her lips, demanding she respond to him.

Miriam felt the little needles of pleasure his kisses had always induced, tiny electric currents she knew from experience would increase and increase until she was helpless and mindless under his sexual expertise. As a throbbing heat began to creep through her body she tried to pull away but he merely shifted his position in response to the half-hearted attempt, holding her more firmly and kissing her again and again, his lips creating shudders of desire.

His hands moved to cup her breasts through the thin material of her vest top, his voice husky against her lips as he murmured, 'You aren't wearing a bra...'

The pads of his thumbs traced an erotic circle round her nipples, bringing the tips into hard peaks, and Miriam moaned; she couldn't help it. Her body aching from the sexual tension of months, she knew she wanted him to make love to her properly. She needed him, she thought raggedly, sucking in a shaky breath as his mouth left hers and moved to her throat and then the swell of her small breasts above the vest top. He was the only man she would ever love and she was only human…

When his hands moved down to her waist and the kisses became lighter she didn't realise at first what was happening. It was only when he raised his head and stepped back slightly, still holding her, that she understood he had stopped his lovemaking. Trembling, she stared at him. The hard, handsome face was showing the faintest trace of colour across his chiselled cheekbones but apart from that he was totally controlled.

She didn't ask him why he had stopped. She didn't have to. Jay provided the answer when he said softly, 'We're not going down that route for now; I don't intend to give you any more ammunition to use against me.'

'What?' She continued to stare at him, her eyes cloudy with desire and her hands clenched at her sides to prevent herself reaching for him.

'It would be so easy to take you to bed this minute.' He took another step away from her, turning and sitting down at the table again, his long legs stretched out in front of him as he surveyed her broodingly. 'But it would be a temporary thing, wouldn't it? And afterwards you'd tell yourself I used sex as a weapon to get you back, to control you or any of the other crimes laid at my door. You see, I'm beginning to understand the way your mind works, my love.'

She wanted to come back at him with an acidic retort to put him in his place but all she could manage was to say weakly, 'You flatter yourself if you think it would be easy to take me to bed, Jay. I've absolutely no intention of sleeping with you again.'

A faintly sardonic expression curled the firm mouth. 'I

could shatter that argument to smithereens in moments and we both know it.'

His male ego was colossal, she thought bitterly. Unfortunately in this case she couldn't afford to challenge him and put it to the test because the last minutes had proved she couldn't trust herself where Jay was concerned. It was humiliating but it appeared she couldn't match him in the self-control game. And this *was* just a game to Jay, she told herself. He had never had the experience of a woman leaving *him* before. Before he had met her the boot had always been on the other foot. Jay had been the typical love-'em-and-leave-'em male animal, as he himself had admitted.

'Sex is only one ingredient in a successful marriage,' she said flatly, turning from the lazer-sharp gaze and pouring herself more coffee for something to do to break the cycle of desire that still held her in its grip.

'My sentiment exactly. Arguably the one that knits everything else together but, as we have no problem in that area, it's a moot point,' Jay said calmly. 'It's everything else we need to work on.'

She swallowed the coffee hot and black, not the way she normally drank it but she needed the caffeine boost. When she raised her head and looked at him again he was watching her, the golden eyes unreadable. Her heart lurched drunkenly. He was so handsome, she thought despairingly. So self-assured and together.

She had never meant to fall in love with him; for a little while after they'd met she'd told herself what she was feeling was a temporary attraction, something that would burn itself out very quickly simply because it was so intense. She had known a man like Jay was not for her but at the beginning she'd convinced herself he was interested in a brief, light-hearted romance, no strings attached, as he had been with his other women in the past. And then one day after they'd been seeing each other for a few weeks he had told her he loved her, that what he felt was no passing fancy but the real thing. A forever commitment. She'd thrown herself into his arms and said she felt the same and that had been that. Before she had known it she was walking down the aisle in a frothy creation, orange blossom entwined in her hair and her mother crying happy tears.

Thoughts of her mother caused the suspicion which had been niggling at the back of her mind for the last days to surface. 'Have you been speaking to my mother recently by any chance?' It seemed strange Jay had chosen the very week she'd told her mother she was going to set the divorce in motion to contact her.

For a long moment he studied her face. 'We talk often.'

That didn't surprise her. Far from there being any mother-in-law problems in their marriage, Jay and her mother had had some sort of mutual-admiration society going from day one, Miriam thought acidly. 'I see.'

'What do you see, my formidable little wife?' Jay drawled mockingly, a faint smile twisting his lips.

'She told you I was going to ask for a divorce.'

'Did she?' He settled himself more comfortably on the chair and took another croissant.

'Well, didn't she?' He could do the calm, cool and collected thing better than anyone she knew and it had always had the power to get under her skin.

His expression changed and when she looked into his eyes they were no longer amused. 'Why ask me when you've already made up your mind?' he said, spreading blackcurrant preserve on the pastry. 'You won't believe me if I answer contrary to what you've decided, I know that.'

It was irritating how often he was right. 'It must be nice to know everything about everyone,' Miriam said in a staccato voice.

He refused to get annoyed. 'It is.' He finished the croissant, licking his fingers appreciatively.

Miriam's eyes followed the action and something hot and pleasurable flickered in the core of her. She remembered the times his mouth had pleasured her to the point of oblivion and shivered. Her voice sharp, she said, 'I don't want to be rude but I've got masses to do today. If you've said all you intended to say…'

'I haven't even begun to get started.' He gave the crooked grin that was so familiar to her. 'But we've all day to talk.'

'All day?' she echoed before pulling herself together. 'Jay, I don't know why you came here this morning and what you're thinking but, like I said, I'm busy this weekend.'

He had reached her and pulled her into his arms seemingly in one fluid movement, kissing her until she was breathless. 'I'm your husband, Miriam. We haven't seen each other before last night for months. Surely you can spare a few hours to discuss issues that will affect the rest of our lives?'

She could never think when he was touching her. Jerking herself free, she muttered, 'What will it take to convince you it's over?'

'You spending some time with me like I said last night.'

She stared at him. 'I told you I won't come back to live at the apartment.'

'And I told you I'm quite happy to live here with you.'

'Which is out of the question.'

'So we date.' He smiled, a dangerous smile. 'I court you all over again. Lovely old-fashioned word that, don't you think? Court? But this time we talk, *really* talk, about anything and everything. No hiding, no secrets, no pretending. However unfair or ugly or unreasonable it is, I want to know what you're thinking and you have the right to hear what I'm thinking.'

Fear, the sort of primeval, cold-terror kind, gripped Miriam. Trying to hide the emotion which was as invasive as it was illogical, she attempted sarcasm. 'I think you know exactly what I think of you, Jay. It's why we separated.'

He didn't react. Coolly, he said, 'OK, we'll take it as read you think I'm the kind of slimeball who'd betray his wife just months after they'd married. But let me ask one thing, and remember we're speaking truth here, however it hurts. Did you ever expect our marriage to last, deep down?'

Involuntarily her eyes dropped to her hands, which were twisted together, fingers entwined. By a conscious act of will she made herself relax her fingers one by one and, still with her head bent, she said, 'I thought I did when we got married.'

'And now?'

Painfully, she made herself say it. 'Now I'm not sure.'

'Because?'

Could she give him the honesty he demanded? After a long moment she raised her head and looked into the golden eyes. 'Because now I'm beginning to realise that all along I knew it was too good to last. You're handsome and wealthy and successful and I'm…' She shrugged; she could only take this truth thing so far. 'I'm not like the sort of woman you used to date.'

She'd surprised him, she could read it in the tough face.

After a moment, he said, 'You're head and shoulders above the women I've known before; I've always told you that.'

Yes, he had, but believing it was something else. 'Jay, I'm ordinary.' When he went to speak, she held up her hand. 'No, let me finish. I'm ordinary, I accept that and I don't mind. You're…' She floundered, not knowing how she could make him see without baring her soul. 'If I'd met someone like—' she searched for a nice, nine-to-five kind of man, someone they both knew '—Jayne's husband, it would have been different.'

'Guy?' He stared at her, nonplussed. 'Why? What's he got that I haven't?'

'It's not what Guy's got—just the opposite. Don't get me wrong,' she added hastily, 'I think he's lovely and perfect for your sister, but when he walks into a room no one notices. Other women, I mean. He hasn't got…oh, I don't know. Charisma, I suppose.' And toe-curling sex-appeal and a hundred other attributes besides, starting with jet-black hair and tawny eyes with the longest lashes she'd ever seen on anyone, and finishing in a perfectly honed, lean, muscled body that would win prizes in any competition.

Those same eyes had now narrowed into golden slits of light. 'You're saying I set out to make myself noticed by other women?'

'No.' She wasn't. Throwing caution to the wind, she said quietly, 'Jay, you must know you're one of the most handsome men on the planet; you don't need to try and get yourself noticed, women fall over themselves for *you* to notice *them*.' Women like Belinda Poppins, for instance.

'Let me get this straight,' he said calmly. Too calmly. 'You're saying our marriage is over because of the way I look?'

Over-simplification but partly true none the less. 'Of course not,' she denied ineffectually. 'Not just that. You're handsome and rich and...' She shrugged. And irresistible.

'I can't help the way I look, Miriam.'

'No, I know that.'

'And I've worked my butt off to get where I am today.'

She nodded. 'I know that too.' He was angry, furious. So much for speaking the truth.

She didn't say the words out loud but she might just as well have. She watched as he read her thoughts in the uncanny way he often had and, as comprehension dawned, Jay smiled wryly. 'OK,' he drawled lazily as the iron self-control kicked in. 'I think that one comes under the heading of unfair *and* unreasonable but you could say I asked for it and the rule still holds. The truth, the whole truth and nothing but the truth. So...' He surveyed her indolently for a moment. 'Other than disfigure myself, lose all I've worked for and end up on the breadline and generally become a bum, how do you see this being reconciled?'

She didn't.

Again he read her mind. 'Oh, no, Miriam,' he said softly. 'Not an option. Not in my book.'

She stared at him, a mixture of pain and defiance on her face. She couldn't go through the last months again, not for anything. She had survived, just, but a second time would tear her into little pieces and there would be a second time. And a third, a fourth...

'OK, we make a deal.' His tone was suddenly brisk, cold, almost distant. 'We see each other until Christmas. If by then you haven't changed your mind, if you still want a divorce, I'll back off and do things your way.'

'You mean it?' She felt worse than she'd felt in the

whole of her life, even the moment she'd seen Jay and Belinda together. But it was what she wanted, wasn't it? What had to be.

'I never say anything I don't mean, that's what you don't understand. Not yet.' He lifted a hand and stroked a lock of hair from her cheek, allowing it to fall back into the silky curtain framing her face. 'But you will, Miriam. You will.' He turned, reaching for his jacket.

'You're leaving?' she asked, confused.

'I'm going to wait for you in the car.' He shrugged into the jacket. 'We're going out for the day. Lunch. Dinner. The whole caboodle. So I presume you want to change. As your home is a little…confined, and we've agreed to keep this relationship on a platonic footing for now, I thought you'd appreciate my waiting downstairs. Am I right?'

'You…you don't have to.' She didn't know if she was on foot or horseback. 'It won't take me long to change.'

'Which will involve you taking off your clothes,' he said lazily. 'And I'm only human, my love.'

And with that he left.

CHAPTER FIVE

How had it come about that she'd agreed to spend the day with Jay?

After he had left the bedsit Miriam stood for a full minute in a state of numb disbelief.

Had she agreed to it? she asked herself once she'd come to life and begun to get ready. She wasn't sure, but somehow it had happened. Which showed nothing had changed. Jay *always* got what he wanted.

She pressed her hands to her hot cheeks, disgusted with herself for the feeling of excitement that was sending tingles down her spine. In spite of everything the thought of spending time with Jay was intoxicating, which was double confirmation she shouldn't be doing it. She wanted to be over him. She wanted to be cool and contained and oblivious to his charm, but wanting wasn't enough. In the aftermath of their separation, when she had been raw and bleeding inside, she'd promised herself she would keep a mental as well as physical distance from Jay. If she didn't let him get near he couldn't hurt her again. Basic common sense. But she hadn't bargained for common sense going out of the window as soon as she was with him.

Groaning, she surveyed the contents of her wardrobe.

What to wear for a day out with one's estranged husband? She didn't want him to think she was trying too hard, but neither did she want to look like the poor relation. Jay hadn't been dressed up, but then he was the sort of man who looked fantastic in anything, so that was no help.

Eventually she decided on a coffee-coloured wool dress and waist-length cashmere cardigan in soft cream. She'd recently treated herself to a pair of cream suede boots and a matching hooded coat for the winter, and in spite of the sunshine outside it was cold enough to wear them. She left her hair loose and applied the minimum of make-up, just mascara and lip gloss, and a pair of plain silver hoops in her ears.

Before leaving the bedsit she looked at herself in the mirror. The high-heeled boots made her legs look longer and slimmer than usual and although the coat had cost a fortune it had been worth it. For once she didn't look too bad, she thought, tilting her head at the bright-eyed girl looking back at her. She didn't possess the smooth sophistication that clothed women like Belinda Poppins, but then she'd never pretended to be a model type.

'Anyway, it doesn't matter how you look,' she muttered, reaching for her handbag. Although it did. Where Jay was concerned, it did. Sighing at her inconsistency, she left the flat.

When she reached the hall, Clara's front door opened. Clara surveyed her accusingly. 'Tell me I'm wrong,' she said dramatically. 'Tell me the reason slimeball is sitting in his car outside is not because he's waiting for you.'

Miriam smiled; she couldn't help it. 'We're going out to lunch,' she admitted, deciding not to mention dinner. 'There are things to discuss.'

Clara rolled her eyes. 'A lamb to the slaughter.'

'No, it's all right, really. I know what I'm doing.'

'With a man like your ex? Honey, no woman knows what she's doing around someone like him. He'll convince you black is white and before you know it you'll be waking up beside him and washing his socks.'

'Not me,' Miriam said as lightly as she could manage. 'I'm done with the whole washing-socks scenario.'

'Now, some of your friends might believe that but not me.' Clara surveyed her darkly, hands on hips. 'You just watch yourself, OK? That soft centre of yours is a mite too soft for your own good at times.'

'OK, Mum.' Miriam smiled. 'See you later.'

When she opened the door of the building the street was lit with a cold, wintry sunshine and Jay immediately unfolded himself from the silver Aston Martin parked in front of the house. By the time she'd reached the car he had the passenger door open for her, his eyes warm as they stroked golden light over her face. 'You look delicious,' he murmured. 'Good enough to eat.'

Miriam frowned. 'I'd prefer to keep this more... platonic if you don't mind,' she said, using his own terminology against him.

His smile was merely a twitch. 'Impossible. I've agreed to keep my lecherous hands off you but that's as far as it goes.'

She stared at him uncertainly, seeing the smoky amusement in his eyes but not knowing how to deal with it. Hiding behind disapproval, she kept the frown on her face as she slid into the beautiful car, the smell of soft leather and the faintest whiff of Jay's aftershave as he bent to shut the door enfolding her in a sensual bubble.

She watched him as he walked round the bonnet to the driver's side, her stomach muscles clenching at his male beauty. And he was beautiful, she thought bleakly—not that Jay would appreciate being labelled such. But his virile good looks and lean muscled body were only part of it; he had a raw animal grace, a magnetism that was something apart from his physical attractiveness and which was very powerful. The more so because he was genuinely unaware of it.

She had been foolish to agree to spend the day with him, Clara was right. She kept her gaze looking straight ahead as Jay joined her in the car. And even more foolish to fall in with seeing him until Christmas. But knowing Jay he wouldn't have taken no for an answer so she'd had little option but to agree. Anyway, she wasn't going to struggle with the whys and wherefores any more. She *had* agreed and that was that. And once the year was over the divorce could steam ahead.

She swallowed hard, trying to ignore the empty sensation that had washed over her.

'Relax, Miriam.' Rather than start the car Jay twisted in his seat to face her, one arm sliding along the back of her seat. 'This isn't supposed to be some sort of endurance test.'

The tender quality to his voice was nearly her undoing. Sternly resisting the temptation to look at him, she said flatly, 'I had rather a lot planned for today, that's all.'

She didn't have to look at him to know he'd seen through the lie. The evidence was in his over-solicitous voice when he said, 'I'm sure you'll soon catch up with everything; you're that sort of person, after all.'

She darted a quick glance under her eyelashes. He was smiling a slow, lazy smile and his eyes were dancing. Reluctantly her lips turned upwards at the corners.

'That's better.' He deposited a swift kiss on her nose and

started the car. 'Today is a step back in time, all right? We've just met, we don't know a thing about each other and we've all the time in the world to find out.'

Warning signals went off loud and clear. 'I don't think—'

'Good. Don't think.' He swung the car out into the road. 'Just let your heart rule your head for once.'

For once? Miriam stared at the chiselled profile. Looking back, that was what she'd always done where Jay was concerned. And look where it had got her. 'Jay, I think it's only fair to tell you I won't change my mind about things,' she said quietly.

'OK, you've told me.' His voice was expressionless. 'So now you can relax. Who knows, you might even enjoy yourself?'

That was exactly what she was worried about.

They lunched at a picturesque little pub on the outskirts of London, a quaint old coaching inn that was all oak beams and brasses and which had a roaring fire in the massive seventeenth-century fireplace. The steak and ale pie was wonderful, as was the apple crumble and custard which followed, and although Miriam kept telling herself all through the meal that she mustn't let her guard down for a minute it was impossible not to with Jay being so amusing and non-threatening. She knew he'd purposely set himself out to be so but it didn't make any difference.

After lunch they went for a walk along the riverbank in the cold, bright air, the blue sky flecked with white clouds and the last of the autumn's leaves fluttering in the icy breeze. A ubiquitous magpie cocked his shiny head at them as they passed, and blackbirds, thrushes and sparrows argued over little insects and seeds in the undergrowth.

Jay had taken her hand early on and she had let it remain in his but, although she expected him to try and kiss her in the quiet and solitude of the wintry afternoon, he didn't. Not even when they made their way back to the pub and Jay's car as dusk flared across the sky in a blaze of pink and gold, turning the evening shadows into vibrant mauve and burnt orange, did he take her in his arms.

As he helped her into the car she was aware of a definite feeling of anticlimax, even testiness, which she knew was monumentally unreasonable.

'What's the matter now?'

Too late she realised her face had betrayed her as he joined her in the car, turning to survey her with narrowed eyes.

'Nothing.' She wiped her face clear of expression.

'I thought we'd had a pleasant afternoon?'

'We have.'

'Damn it, Miriam.' He sighed in exasperation. 'I've trodden on eggshells all day but clearly something's wrong and I'm not in the mood to play games.'

'Nor am I.' She could have kicked herself for not hiding her feelings better. Jay had always been like a radar as far as her emotions were concerned, picking up on things almost before she was aware of them herself. 'I've told you, everything's fine.'

The pub was one of those that served meals all day and evening and the car park was quite full. As a family saloon crawled up behind them and then sat waiting for their space, she said, 'Are we going?'

'Not until you tell me what put that look on your face.'

She hesitated, then decided to tell half the truth. The less humiliating half. 'This afternoon's reminded me of how it used to be, that's all, before—' She stopped abruptly. 'Before we split up.' She had been going to say before Belinda but somehow she couldn't bear to say the other woman's name at this moment in time. Not with the setting sun creating a river of colour in the charcoal-blue sky and the scent of his body warmth just inches away.

'Good. Then it's achieved what I wanted.' His eyes held hers, very steady, very calm. 'And I don't intend to apologise for it.'

She stared at him, taken aback. She knew he could be as hard as nails when he had to be but he'd never been that way with her. Now, though, there was an uncompromising note in his voice, his tone reminiscent of her mother's when she was using her 'you have to be cruel to be kind' argument. Raising her chin slightly, Miriam said, 'I wouldn't expect you to, not the great Jay Carter, who's never wrong.'

He looked at her, one eyebrow rising in a way that made Miriam feel like a petulant child. 'I can make mistakes like the next person,' he said quietly. 'I made one of the biggest ten months ago. I should have come and fetched you home that first night and made love to you until you knew without a shadow of a doubt that you're the only woman in my life.'

A warmth spread through her and she licked suddenly dry lips. 'The car that's waiting is getting impatient,' she said in an attempt to change the conversation.

'Let it.' His eyes gently mocked her.

She felt hot with a mixture of embarrassment and something else, something she didn't want to put a name to. Thankfully Jay didn't prolong the moment too long, turning from her and starting the car. 'You're one of the few women I know who can still blush,' he said lazily as they left the pub and turned onto the road beyond the car park. 'It's incredibly sexy.'

'Turning lobster-red? I don't think so.' Miriam forced a laugh.

'But then I find everything about you incredibly sexy,' he continued as though she hadn't spoken. 'Your soft skin, the way your freckles pepper that skin like delicious ginger spice…'

'Jay, please—'

'Finding each freckle with my mouth, my tongue… Do you remember?' he asked softly. 'Do you dream about us making love in our big bed till dawn? Pleasing each other, drunk with the intoxication that comes from being loved and loving in return? Do you think of those times, Miriam?'

'No,' she lied. 'No, I don't.'

'I do. All the time, especially at night. And cold showers don't help at all, do you know that? Nothing does.' He took one of her hands, his finger sliding against her curved palm and tracing up a crease to her wrist.

Miriam fought against showing how his touch affected her but as tingles shot up her arm she pulled her hand away. 'Don't,' she said sharply. 'Not when you're driving.'

His gaze hadn't moved from the road ahead and it didn't now, a thread of laughter in his voice when he said, 'And when I'm not driving? What then? No, don't answer that. I can look but not touch, right?'

'I didn't set that rule.' She regretted the words as soon as they were voiced. They said far too much.

'No, you're right, you didn't,' he murmured thoughtfully. 'Why was that, I wonder? Could it be you want me as much as I want you?'

She stiffened. 'In your dreams,' she bit out fiercely.

'Oh, now, if we're going on to our dreams that's a whole new ball game.' His voice was very dry. 'My dreams are definitely of the X-rated variety where you're concerned. How about yours?'

Hers had caused her to blush in the cold light of day and taught her she didn't know herself as well as she had thought.

'I rarely dream anything worth remembering,' she said crisply.

'I can always tell when you're lying.'

'Your list of accomplishments is amazing,' she said with heavy sarcasm, 'but in this case wishful thinking.'

Jay shook his head slowly. 'I don't think so.'

She dragged her eyes away from the handsome face, staring out of the windscreen like Jay. Her heart felt like a tight ball in her chest. 'You don't know me at all or you'd have known I wouldn't tolerate another person in our marriage.'

'Miriam, there's always been a third person in our marriage.' Darkness was falling quickly, lights gleaming in the windows of houses they were passing. Somehow the cosy quality to the scene outside the car made her feel ten times worse.

She glanced at him again. 'What's that supposed to mean?'

'The spectre of your father has been there from the word go; I was just too dim to realise before.'

She reared up as though she'd been stung. 'My father has absolutely nothing to do with us. He was dead long before I met you.'

'He was handsome and charming but quite ruthless, wasn't he?' Jay went on. 'I've had a couple of interesting chats with your mother about him recently. She showed me a photograph she'd kept of him. He had a weak mouth.'

She opened her mouth to deny it but then she realised Jay was right. She wondered why she'd never noticed it before.

'I've never trusted men with weak mouths,' Jay said softly. 'Or women, come to that. It's the one feature that betrays the inner person.'

'This is all very interesting but I repeat, my father has nothing to do with us.'

'Wrong. He has *everything* to do with where we are now.' It was swift and inflexible. 'And the way I feel about him it's fortunate he's dead.'

There were a few moments of awkward silence. Miriam didn't know what to say to break it; there had been a very real controlled rage in Jay's voice that had shocked her.

'But there it is,' Jay said quietly after a little while, his voice expressionless now. 'I'm fighting against the legacy of a ghost but at least I have a better understanding of why now.'

'Why?'

'Why you're like you are, why your boyfriends before me were the type of spineless individuals who were looking for a mother rather than a girlfriend, men who were content to be led by a ring through their nose.'

'Don't be ridiculous.' She was mortally offended.

'But then you fell in love,' he went on remorselessly. 'The last thing you'd bargained for or wanted. The safety net was gone. Suddenly you understood how your mother had felt about your father and subconsciously the barriers went up. This was forbidden territory, dangerous, like quicksand. One minute your feet were on solid ground, the next you were sinking in a host of emotions you found overwhelming.'

She was shaking. She didn't know if it was because his insight had bulldozed open a door in her mind she'd relentlessly kept closed, or because she was more angry than she'd ever been in the whole of her life. 'Stop this car. I want to get out.'

'You want to run away? Again?' he added grimly.

'I didn't run away. I left you because you'd made it impossible for me to stay by having an affair,' she shouted back. Loudly.

'You believed what you'd schooled yourself to believe. What you had willed would happen one day. Deep in your mind it was just a matter of time.'

'I *saw* you.' Only the fact Jay was driving prevented her from hitting him. As this knowledge registered it served like a bucket of icy cold water over her head. Miriam had always considered herself the gentlest of souls, but right at this moment if she could have really hurt him she knew she would have done so.

What was she turning into? she asked herself, horrified. What had *he* turned her into? She drew in a long silent breath. 'I'd like to go home now, please.'

He glanced at her white face and the next moment she was aware they were turning off the brightly lit main road into a quieter tree-lined side-road. As he cut the engine he turned, taking her into his arms before she had time to object. He kissed her as she struggled against him and after a minute or two she stopped fighting him. It was only then he raised his head to say softly, 'You *are* home, Miriam, here in my arms. It's just a matter of believing it, that's all.'

'I can't.' She felt too emotionally drained to argue.

'You will.' He sounded so sure, so confident that she felt a second's sharp anger spear the weariness. 'But for now no more talking. We're going to the theatre tonight—I've got the tickets here—and then for a meal at Ravencrofts, where I've reserved a quiet table for two tucked away in a secluded alcove.'

She raised her eyes, her gaze holding his for an infinitesimal moment. 'It's no good, Jay. You know that in the heart of you, don't you? We can't go back to the way things were.'

'I don't want to go back to how it was.' There was a significant pause before he added, 'This time you're going to give me your whole heart, Miriam. I want you body, soul and spirit—nothing else will do.'

CHAPTER SIX

MIRIAM woke up at six o'clock the next morning, long before her alarm was due to go off. Unusually for her she was instantly wide awake, although she remained curled under the duvet as she reviewed every minute of the day before, her heart beating faster as she pictured Jay's hard, handsome face on the screen of her mind.

The theatre seats had been for a show she'd been longing to see for ages but for which she'd been unable to get tickets, it being booked solid for months ahead. Needless to say, Jay had secured a couple of the best seats in the house along with champagne and strawberries served in their box in the interval. He had dropped off the car in the company car park and hailed a taxi to the theatre, and when they'd emerged from the show another taxi had been waiting to take them to Ravencrofts, an exclusive and very expensive restaurant in the heart of London's West End.

The meal had been wonderful and he had been the epitome of congenial dinner companion, keeping the conversation light and amusing. When he had taken her home he'd kept the taxi waiting while he saw her to her front door, and although this time he had kissed her goodnight it had been a friendly, undemanding kiss and he had left immediately.

And today she was seeing him again. Miriam sat up in bed at the thought, wrapping her arms round her knees as she considered her stupidity. And it *was* stupid to play with fire. She rocked back and forth a couple of times before snuggling under the covers again as the chill in the room struck. The heating wasn't due to come on for another hour.

In the quietness of the room Jay's words of the day before played in her head over and over again. She had been too emotionally and mentally exhausted the night before to do more than shower and fall into bed, but now her mind was like a dog with a bone. Away from the piercing tawny eyes she allowed herself to consider what he'd said about her father and her attitude to love and the male species. She had always told herself she had attracted a certain type of man because she was too soft, and lame ducks, men who had needed her to look after them to some extent and take charge, had seemed to recognise this. Now she found herself wondering if rather than them seeking her out, she had been the one to instigate her previous relationships before Jay. Could he be right? Had she subconsciously been making sure she was always the one in control of the relationship? Certainly she had never felt the slightest inclination to get serious with any of them.

She tossed and turned under the duvet, the nature of her musing making her uncomfortable and irritable. Even with that in mind, it still didn't alter what Jay had done, she told herself after a contemplative half-hour. In fact it only proved she had been right not to get involved with the handsome, charming, love-'em-and-leave-'em types in the past.

Although Jay hadn't loved her and left her, not really.

The thought came out of the blue and propelled her out

of bed regardless of the cold. Pulling on her bathrobe, she decided on an early-morning soak but once she was lying in the warm water she found herself thinking about him again. He had always insisted on his innocence and had never written them off as a couple. It had been her who'd done that.

With good reason, another part of her mind argued. She had virtually caught him in the act with Belinda, for goodness' sake. And then the woman had confirmed all her fears when she had spoken about their affair. Why would Belinda have done that if she hadn't been sleeping with Jay?

Jealousy? the first voice suggested. A woman scorned and all that. The green-eyed monster was a powerful one.

She lay back in the soapy water, her head whirling as something like panic gripped her. She couldn't rethink all this, she *couldn't*. Not just because she had been with Jay yesterday and fallen under his spell. Clara had said he could convince her black was white and Clara was right.

'I know what I know.' She said the words out loud because she needed to hear them. If she started doubting herself now it would mean the last miserable ten months had been for nothing, that *she* was the one at fault. And she wasn't. Jay had made her out to be some sort of headcase yesterday, when she thought about it, with all that talk concerning her father. What was that if not controlling? Well, she wasn't going to be manipulated.

She sat up sharply in the water, causing a wave to swish over onto the tiled floor. She had to be resolute and true to herself. She couldn't let herself become nothing more than a puppet, dancing to Jay's tune.

Clara knocked on her door at nine o'clock, still in her nightie and bathrobe—black, obviously—and looking curiously childlike without the outrageous eye make-up and with her hair as yet unspiked for the day. Bounding into the bedsit like an eager puppy, she plumped herself down on the floor after dragging a cushion off the sofa. 'Right, all the gory details, please,' she demanded serenely.

Miriam smiled. 'Sorry to disappoint but he was the perfect gentleman.'

'*Again?*' Clara wrinkled her small nose. 'You mean he didn't try and have his wicked way with you?'

Miriam shook her head.

'So what did you do? Where did you go? When are you seeing him again?'

'We had lunch, a walk by the river, went to the theatre and then dinner and I'm seeing him again in exactly—' Miriam made a show of glancing at her wristwatch '—two hours.'

'You are? Oh, *Miriam.*' Clara shook her head in despair. 'I knew it. He's reeled you in again.'

'He most certainly has not.'

Bright blue eyes met soft brown. 'Are you sure about that?'

'Absolutely.'

'And there are no interesting details of the kiss-and-tell variety?'

'None.' She had decided to draw a veil over that blistering kiss before they'd left the bedsit yesterday.

'Well, put the coffee on and I'll tell you something really funny.'

Miriam looked more closely at her friend. There had been a note in Clara's voice she couldn't place; something between excited and sheepish was the best way to describe it. 'What's happened?'

Clara shifted on the cushion, looking down at her hands,

which were playing with the corded edging as she said, 'You know that guy I told you about? The one I've been talking to at work?'

'The one who's—' Miriam had been going to say celibate but changed it to, 'in tune with himself?'

Clara nodded. 'We're seeing each other.'

Miriam busied herself with the coffee, keeping her voice casual as she said, 'So why is that funny?'

'You'll know when you see him. Not that there's anything the matter with him,' Clara added quickly, 'there's not, he's—he's great, but very…establishment. You know?'

Miriam wasn't quite sure she did. 'Establishment?'

Clara waved a black-taloned hand. 'You *know*, suit and tie, polished shoes, drives to the speed limit and is good to his mother, that sort of thing.'

Miriam handed Clara her coffee. 'Oh,' she said.

'Exactly.' Clara's voice was verging on a wail. 'I mean, me with someone like that. It's ridiculous.'

'But you like him,' Miriam said carefully, sitting down on the remaining cushion on the sofa and taking a sip of coffee.

Clara nodded.

'And he likes you?'

If she hadn't seen it with her own eyes Miriam would have said it was impossible, but Clara actually went pink as she said, 'He says he does.'

Miriam thought for a moment. 'Well, look at it like this. You've always gone for edgy, shall we say somewhat… outrageous types, yes? Which with the way you are is probably to be expected. By going out with someone like…'

'Brian,' Clara supplied.

'Really? Brian?' Miriam couldn't think of a more circumspect name. 'OK, by going out with Brian you're actually breaking away from tradition. For you, that is.'

Clara's eyes lit up. 'I hadn't looked at it like that.'

'And he's probably doing the same. I bet he hasn't gone out with anyone like you before.' In fact, Miriam could guarantee it. And that without meeting the man.

Clara grinned. 'You'd better believe it. His last girl-friend was the tweeds-and-pearls type and had an "honourable" before her name.'

Miriam found she couldn't wait to see this Brian.

By the time Clara left after several cups of coffee and a plate of toast it was ten-thirty. Miriam just had time to change into smart black trousers and a bubblegum-pink top and do her make-up before the buzzer told her Jay had arrived.

She found her heart was racing as she hurried down the stairs and stopped abruptly. Taking several deep, calming breaths, she then proceeded at a more sedate pace and, once in the hall, walked steadily to the front door. When she opened it Jay was standing on the pavement talking to a tall young man with a short, neat haircut and spectacles and very polished shoes.

Jay's face was absolutely deadpan when he looked at her. 'This is Brian Mason—he's here to see Clara.'

His careful lack of expression told Miriam he found the situation hilarious. Miriam ignored the wicked glitter in his eyes and directed her gaze at Brian. Smiling, she said, 'Hi, I'm Miriam, Clara's friend from the top floor. Is she expecting you?'

Brian smiled at her, revealing pearly white teeth and dimples. Miriam could immediately see what had captured Clara. There was something terribly ingenuous about that smile; not naive exactly, more honest and sincere.

'I said I'd pop round at some point today,' said Brian, nervously adjusting his scarf more securely into the lapels of his overcoat, 'but if it's not convenient…'

'I'm sure she's in. Wait just a minute and I'll check.' Miriam left the pair of them and darted across the hall, knocking on Clara's front door.

When her friend opened it she was still in her nightie and bathrobe. 'Brian's on the doorstep.' Miriam gestured behind her. 'He's talking to Jay.'

'Brian?' Clara was suddenly all of a dither, which was a first. 'But I haven't done my hair or anything.'

'You look lovely,' Miriam said with sincerity. In fact, she thought Clara *au naturel*, with her face free from layers of make-up and her hair softly framing her sweet face, might test Brian's vow of celibacy to the limit, even without the added titillation of the black nightie. 'Shall I tell him to come in?'

Clara nodded, still flustered. 'The place is a mess.'

'When isn't your place a mess?'

'True, but Brian's so tidy. You only have to see his desk at work to know that.'

'And I bet your desk is like the bedsit, so don't worry. It's *you* he likes or he wouldn't be here.'

Outside the two men were chatting away quite easily when Miriam called Brian to say Clara was at home, and once she was sitting beside Jay in the car she asked curiously, 'What were you and Brian talking about?'

Jay leant across and kissed her soundly. 'First things first,' he murmured softly. 'Good morning, Mrs Carter.'

Miriam's heart quickened, her senses instantly alight. The kiss hadn't been overtly sensual but his words were like a warm, intimate stroking of her whole being. Shakily, she responded, 'Good morning.'

'Good morning, Mr Carter,' he corrected with a lazy smile, his eyes dancing as they mocked her pink confusion. 'I'm your husband, remember?'

'Isn't that rather a formal way to talk to your husband?' Miriam managed with a brave attempt at nonchalance.

'Absolutely,' he agreed immediately. 'If it's intimacy you're looking for—'

'I'm not,' she cut him off quickly.

'Of course, what I'd like to begin the day is the feel of your body beneath mine,' he continued as though she hadn't spoken, his voice slow and deep. 'Naked, silky, warm. I'd like to look at you, kiss you all over, feel you shudder and sigh and breathe my name as I make love to you. I'd like to touch and caress you and bring you to fever-pitch, make your flesh quiver and tremble. Remember how it used to be, Miriam? You used to make me as hard as a rock when you quivered beneath my tongue and hands.'

'Don't.' It was a whisper.

'And when we'd sated each other's needs we'd lie joined together and kiss and talk until we did it all over again,' he went on relentlessly. 'Because we weren't just sexual partners, Miriam. We were one. Joined in every way. Until you came into my life I had slept with women, never *loved* them. There's a difference.'

She wanted to tell him to stop, that he was being unfair, but she couldn't utter a sound. In Jay's eyes there was no mockery, no teasing, only a deep, unnerving tenderness. And against such she had no defence.

He moved away slightly but still kept his hand against the side of her face, his fingers playing with the soft, silky fall of her hair as though he couldn't quite break contact with her. 'Are you beginning to search yourself?' he asked quietly, his eyes still on her face. 'Or are you still hiding from the past?'

'I—I don't know what you mean.' She couldn't do this. Not here, not now.

He observed her in silence, waiting. After a long few moments he sighed. 'I love you. I've always loved you. And loving you means being faithful in my book. When I took my vows it wasn't on a whim, Miriam. We weren't two young kids. I knew from the first date that you weren't the sort of woman to just have fun with for a while, that it would be all or nothing. And I chose all.'

Her throat was locked and she was incapable of speaking. She met his gaze in numb despair. She wanted to believe him. If it was just a matter of wanting she would throw herself into his arms and tell him exactly what he wanted to hear. But it would be a lie.

His lips caressed hers. After a moment he said softly, 'I don't know what else to say.'

Her eyes filled with tears. 'I—I don't want you to say anything.'

The sky had clouded over in the last hour and now the first drops of sleety rain splattered against the windscreen. She felt cold. Inside and out, she felt cold. Helplessly she clenched her hands into fists. 'It would have been better for both of us if we hadn't seen each other again,' she whispered miserably. 'This is just dragging out the inevitable.'

'The only inevitable I'm prepared to consider is you in my arms where you belong, and this time for good.' He drew back into his seat, starting the engine. 'And however painful the process for us to get there, so be it.'

For a fleeting moment she wondered what it must be

like to be so completely sure of yourself. She had never been that way, ever. 'And if we don't? Get there, I mean.'

'We will,' Jay said with infuriating calmness as the windscreen wipers battled with lumps of ice and he drew away from the house. 'You're mine and I don't let go of what's mine.'

Suddenly Miriam was angry. 'Like your car or the business or the apartment, you mean?'

A muscle twitched in Jay's jaw. 'I'm not going to grace that question with an answer.'

'Because the truth might incriminate you?' she retorted.

'Because it's not worthy of a reply.'

Miriam opened her mouth to argue further but something in the set of Jay's hard face warned her she'd pushed him as far as she could. He looked like thunder, she thought shakily. She didn't think she had ever seen him quite so furious.

It was a full ten minutes later, a ten minutes fraught with electricity, before she said in a small voice, 'Where are we going?'

'We're having a culture day.' He glanced at her briefly. 'The National Gallery opens at noon and after that we'll take a late lunch. There's a craft gallery that stays open late on a Sunday I'd like you to see, and we're eating Italian tonight. OK?'

Nothing was OK. He must know that. Her silence was an unspoken answer.

'I can't recall you being so grumpy in the past,' Jay observed mildly. 'You used to laugh all the time.'

'I've changed,' she said flatly. Adultery had a way of taking all the amusement out of life.

'No, I don't think so. You just need to chill out, relax.'

He was something else, he really was! 'I chill out often,'

Miriam said, trying hard to keep the outrage out of her voice. 'And walking about with a gormless smile plastered on my face has never been my style actually.'

'You couldn't look gormless if you tried.'

His smile was singularly sweet and swept away her resentment in a moment of time. Telling herself she was being subjected to the Carter charm, she managed to keep her voice cool and even when she said, 'Thank you. I'm afraid we might have to skip dinner tonight, Jay. I've things to do before work in the morning.'

'Like washing your hair?' he asked drily.

'And some cleaning and a spot of ironing and so on.'

'I've always believed that domestic chores shouldn't rule one, so sorry, not a good enough excuse. Dinner's still on.'

He'd always believed domestic chores shouldn't rule one? Well, that was a mite easy for a man who employed a daily. Her voice studiously polite, Miriam said, 'And how is Mrs Rowan, by the way?'

'Still asking when you're coming home.'

She perhaps should have expected that one. Knowing she would never win in a war of words, Miriam turned to look out of the window at the grey streets and folk scurrying about under umbrellas. It didn't matter what he said or did in the long run, all she had to do was to remain resolute. There were only a few weeks until Christmas and she didn't doubt Jay would keep his word and make the divorce as smooth as possible when she still wanted one when the time was up. She just had to be strong. Her soft mouth set in a determined line. And she would be. Just as walking about with a gormless smile plastered on her face wasn't her style, neither was emotional suicide.

CHAPTER SEVEN

OVER the following weeks Miriam found her resolution to stay emotionally detached was severely tried. A cold, wet autumn had given way to bright, crisp days with thick white frosts at night, and winter had definitely arrived. As the gusts of a chill November wind saw the month out, December came in with a glinting sparkle on spider webs and the crunch of frosty ground. She had been dreading this month all year, knowing echoes of the Christmas the year before would feature even more vividly in her dreams. As it was, with seeing Jay every evening and at the weekends and coping with a demanding job, the changing of the month was merely a date on letterheads.

She made concentrated efforts to take each day as it came and to keep some mental space between her and Jay, but it was hard. Especially when they were together. A strange feeling was taking hold of her but she repressed it, refusing to acknowledge the weakness that told her she couldn't do without him. She could. She had. And she'd have to in the future. It was as simple as that. Anything else was impossible.

She knew Jay was playing the waiting game, thinking she would change her mind about the divorce the more they became inseparable. And they were. Every minute they weren't working they were together, but Jay always went home at night.

Several times in the last weeks, when he had kissed her with single-minded intensity and she was limp with raging desire, she had expected he would take their lovemaking to the next level. But he had never so much as undone one button on her clothes, let alone undressed her.

She knew he wanted to. He never missed an opportunity to touch her or take her hand and his compliments were seductive and sexy. And he certainly wasn't seeing anyone else, he was always with her. But even though he kissed her until she was senseless that iron control held.

Which was good. Miriam nodded to herself as she finished getting ready for work on the first Monday in December. She and Jay had had a lazy Sunday the day before. He'd arrived at her bedsit with the Sunday papers just after ten o'clock and they'd read them while the Sunday roast cooked in her tiny kitchen area. She had still resolutely refused to visit the apartment again and so inevitably Jay was spending more and more time in her little home. After lunch they'd gone to Hyde Park and walked some calories off before undoing all the good work and having a cream tea at the Brass Kettle, a smart little teashop tucked away in a side-road near Knightsbridge where the waitresses wore black dresses and white aprons and all the food was home-made.

When he'd seen her home just as the winter sun was setting and casting fleeting wisps of silver into the pearly pink sky he had kissed her long and hard with a fierce possessiveness that had made her want more. Much more. And that was bad. Miriam surveyed herself in the mirror before leaving the bedsit. Very bad. She couldn't afford to start sleeping with him. That would take their relationship somewhere it couldn't go, somewhere where she became vulnerable again.

As she came down the stairs Clara emerged from her bedsit on her way to work, her hair all the colours of the rainbow and her lips as black as coal. In the last three weeks she'd had as many new piercings and her clothes were even more outrageous than normal.

'Hi.' Clara's smile was bright but strained. 'Good weekend with slimeball?'

Miriam nodded. 'And you? How are things with Brian?' she asked quietly. She was worried about Clara. When they'd had breakfast together on Saturday her friend had been too sparky, too upbeat, almost brittle.

'Great.' And then Clara stopped with her hand on the front door. 'No, not great. Awful. And it's all my fault. I—I keep pushing him away, saying and doing things to make him go off me.'

Hence the new piercings and psychedelic hair. Miriam stared at her. 'Why?' she asked simply.

'Because I'm not in control any more.' Clara's blue eyes were desperate. 'I don't feel like myself. I'm terrified he'll leave and yet I can't stop doing things to make him do just that. Last night I said some terrible things; I even brought his mother into it and she's such a sweet old biddy.'

Miriam was stunned. Suddenly she realised she was seeing the real Clara, that the easy-going, happy-go-lucky front was just that. A front. 'But you care for him?'

'That's the trouble. I don't want to love anyone. As soon as you do that you leave yourself wide open for a fall.'

'But Brian's crazy about you, Clara. Anyone can see that. He loves you.'

'My parents were supposed to love me but that didn't stop my dad leaving when I was six and then my mum putting me into care. Said she couldn't cope. Ha! With a six-year-old? And the next minute she'd taken up with some fella who had three kids and was looking after them.'

'Oh, Clara.' After all their girly chats and meals together Miriam couldn't believe this was happening on a Monday morning in the hall when they were both on their way to work.

'She had me back for a while when I was eight. The new guy said he wanted us to be a family, that I was to look on him as my dad. I was so grateful to him and so scared I might do or say something to spoil things. And then he came to my room one night when Mum was out...'

Again Miriam said, 'Oh, Clara.' She just didn't know what to do except hug Clara close. When the hug ended both their faces were wet. 'What happened after that? Did you tell your mum?' Miriam asked softly.

'I tried to but she wouldn't listen. She didn't want anything to spoil her new perfect life, I suppose,' Clara said bitterly. 'And he threatened me all the time, saying they'd lock me away if I said anything, that no one would listen to a child. I believed him. If my own mother didn't believe me, why would anyone else? Then when I was ten there was a teacher at school who saw through the rebellious brat I'd become. One day I told her everything. The police were involved and a police doctor confirmed I was speaking the truth. He went to prison but my mother still insisted I was lying and said she wanted nothing more to do with me. I didn't mind being back in care—anything was better than what I'd lived with.'

'I'm so terribly sorry, Clara.'

Clara shrugged, forcing a smile through her tears. 'That's life. The positive thing was I discovered I had a brain, that I was really very bright. At uni I made up my mind I'd make a good life for myself, get a brilliant job and live on my terms. Use men to get what I wanted but no involvement. I mean, who needs it?'

They were both going to be late for work but Miriam knew she couldn't stop Clara talking; her friend's face had looked haunted when she'd first seen her. 'And then Brian came along,' she said softly.

Clara nodded. 'And then Brian came along,' she echoed flatly. 'He told me last night he made up his mind a year ago he was going to be celibate until the right woman, the *one,* came along. He'd slept with other girlfriends since he was seventeen or eighteen but one day he woke up thinking he wanted something different from that.' She shrugged. 'He can be very determined when he makes up his mind about something; he's terrifically good at his job. He—he said last night he knew I was the woman.'

'How did you feel?' Miriam didn't really need to ask; she had seen the desperation on Clara's face that morning.

'Panicky, scared, aggressive.' Clara's heavy eye make-up had already streaked down her cheeks; now she made it worse by scrubbing at her eyes with her fists as she added, 'I was evil, Miriam. I don't think he'll ever talk to me again, let alone want to go out with me.'

'He doesn't know about your mother and what happened with this man?'

Clara shook her head. 'Apart from the teacher and a therapist I had to see when I was in care, I've never discussed this with anyone else but you.'

'You need to tell him, Clara.'

'I couldn't.' Clara started to cry again. 'I know it's daft but he might look at me differently; it would change things. He'd know too much, it'd give him too much power… Oh, I can't explain how I feel.'

Miriam felt at a loss for a moment. Then she took Clara's arm. 'Come on. We're going up to my place and we'll both ring in to work and say we ate something that disagreed with us last night and will be late. You're going to have a coffee and something to eat and we're going to talk this through. OK?'

'I can't.' Clara sniffed miserably. 'I've got to pull some material together for a programme that's already way behind schedule, and because it's of a sensitive nature no one else can take over.'

'Tough.' Miriam was not going to be deflected. 'You're far more important than any TV programme and this is the rest of your life we're talking about here.'

Now Clara smiled weakly. 'True,' she admitted. 'Dramatic, but true.'

Two hours and plenty of tears later, Clara had agreed she'd tell Brian she had something important to discuss with him when she saw him at work, and could they meet later that day? 'But what if he's already decided he's had enough?' she said to Miriam as they repaired their make-up preparatory to leaving the bedsit. 'I was absolutely foul to him last night, and I do mean foul. He might have made up his mind he's sick of being the nice guy to such an out-and-out headcase as me.'

'He won't and you're not,' Miriam said firmly, praying silently her faith in the stalwart Brian wasn't ill-founded. If ever anyone needed a hero, it was Clara.

'I wouldn't blame him.' Clara stopped what she was doing and stared gloomily at her reflection. 'The chances are our relationship won't last anyway—we're from different ends of the spectrum. He had the classically normal upbringing and when his father died five years ago he was devastated. His mother is an absolute love with a heart of gold. He couldn't possibly understand where I'm coming from.'

'You underestimate him.' Miriam turned Clara round by her shoulders to face her. 'And his mum sounds just what you need. I think this has every chance of going the course and you do too, deep down. That's why you've got the jitters.'

Clara raised an eyebrow. 'OK, wise woman. I concede defeat.'

'I'm not wise—far from it. Believe me, Clara, I'm just as messed up as you are but without such good cause.' As she said it her own words reverberated in her head. Fortunately Clara was too immersed in her own problems to dwell on what Miriam had said and the moment passed, but as the two of them made their way downstairs Miriam was telling herself she would think about all the issues Clara's revelations had thrown up later. Much later. Once she was in bed. With a sickening jolt she realised there would be plenty to consider.

In spite of the awfulness of all Clara had confided, Miriam found she wasn't thinking of her friend as she opened the front door of the house. It was Jay who was at the forefront of her mind. Probably because of this the young, bespectacled, shiny-shoed man standing on the pavement didn't register with her until behind her she heard Clara breathe, 'Brian? What are you doing here?'

'You didn't come in this morning and someone said you weren't well.'

'I'm—I'm all right.'

'You've been crying.'

'I know.'

Miriam decided it was a good moment to bow out. Turning to Clara, who had turned an interesting shade of pink, she said, 'I'm sure you two have things to discuss and I must be getting off. See you later.'

She didn't think either of them noticed her leave.

On the way to work she found she was depressed, and—shamefully, she admitted to herself—it wasn't because of the tragic tale Clara had told her. She simply felt very small and very alone, and the only person who could make it better was the one person who couldn't—if that made sense. Which it didn't, of course.

Sighing heavily, she raised her head to see the woman opposite her on the tube staring at her from over the top of her newspaper. By the time Miriam had smiled at her the woman was already reading again, but that was the way it was on the underground. Momentary eye contact and then back to anonymity.

She hated the tube. Miriam glanced round the crowded confines of the train and sighed again, but silently this time. When she'd been with Jay one of the joys of married life had been a lift to work. Not that that was important in the overall scheme of things, she assured herself swiftly, shocked at the blatant materialism. But still, it had been nice...

Her thoughts meandered on with the jolting of the train. So had waking up beside Jay each morning, opening her eyes and seeing his dark head on the pillow; sharing the funny moments that had occurred at their respective work places over dinner; drowning in the scent and feel of the one person in the world who loved you more than life itself—except he hadn't. Or… Her heart began to thud so hard it felt it was jumping out of her throat. Had she made a mistake? *Had* he been telling the truth all along?

Finding she wanted to cry, she hastily pulled herself together and determined to stop thinking about Jay. She didn't know what had got into her this morning; it must be because of Clara. She would never have believed the girl had such a heartbreaking past if she hadn't heard it from Clara herself; Clara was always so cheerful and funny and light-hearted. It just went to show no one ever really knew anyone else.

She did so hope Brian would come up trumps for Clara, but he would, she was sure of it. The look in his eyes when he'd stood staring at Clara this morning had been everything any woman could want. And look how he'd come to find her despite all Clara had said the night before. They'd be fine. He clearly had the sort of tenacity needed to help Clara face and beat her gremlins.

As the train neared her stop she began to run through some of the more important things to do when she reached the office, but try as she might to keep them at bay, truths that had resonated with her because of her own situation crowded her mind. As Clara had talked, revealing her own insecurities, Miriam had known the other girl was inadvertently highlighting more than just her own weaknesses. They were very different, she and Clara, but in some ways disturbingly similar. Clara had chosen a somewhat promiscuous lifestyle involving relationships with men she'd known she wouldn't fall in love with but who presented something of a challenge, dumping them as soon as they'd fallen for her. She, on the other hand, had unconsciously picked needy types who relied on her far more than she did them, mainly because she hadn't been able to trust that they wouldn't leave her unless it was that way. But it all boiled down to the same thing, a need to be in control, to be holding the whip hand. And then she had met Jay.

She shivered, although she wasn't cold. They'd reached her station and she was thankful for it; she didn't want to think any more.

But even as she walked the short distance from the tube station thoughts crowded in. She hadn't meant to fall in love, she had never bargained for it. In fact she didn't really think she had believed in it until it had happened to her. Love, she'd decided very early on in life, was essentially a fierce sexual attraction, a me-Tarzan, you-Jane type of primal magnetism between the sexes. Avoid that and you wouldn't be fooled into the net as her mother had been. Hence, she supposed, her penchant for subconsciously choosing lame ducks.

She stopped at the steps to the building, unaware of desultory flakes of snow whirling in the wind as she stood looking inwards. For the first time she admitted to herself that under the wonder and excitement of Jay sweeping her off her feet, of them getting married, being blissfully happy, there had always been a strong undercurrent of fear. Jay had said it was inevitable they would separate because she'd convinced herself he was like her father and that believing anything else would make her too vulnerable. She didn't think that was wholly true but there was an element of truth in it. She had felt too deeply, loved him too much and it had frightened her, even as she had done everything she could to please him. Like pretending to enjoy living at the apartment because she'd known how much he loved it there.

When the worst had happened, when she had found him

with Belinda and her world had come crashing down about her ears, there had still been a strange feeling of some weight being taken off her shoulders. Now she realised it was because the waiting had finally come to an end.

She made herself walk up the steps into the centrally heated confines of the office block, taking the lift to the floor where Thorpe & Sons operated. As she walked through the outer office to reach her smaller one, which led on to her boss's more spacious domain, one of the girls called to her that Mr Thorpe had left a message to say he'd be back after lunch, should she make it in.

Miriam thanked her, but on reaching her office she closed the door to shut out the low hum of conversation and noise and sat down at her desk without turning on her computer.

Staring ahead, she faced another truth. She had been putting off speaking to Jay's sister for weeks. She knew Jay wanted her to, although he'd made no mention of it since that first night he had taken her out to dinner. He had spoken of Jayne a few times, saying her morning sickness tended to be all day and she was feeling tired but still thrilled about the baby, but that was all.

Her reason for not contacting Jayne wasn't altogether that she didn't want to put Jay's sister in a difficult position, Miriam admitted silently to herself. The trouble was she liked Jayne very much, loved her even; in the short time she'd known her Jayne had become the sister she'd never had. And that was another thread in the sticky web that had trapped her.

Miriam's smooth brow wrinkled with self-derision. Was she really such a mess? It would seem so. Suddenly a whole host of hang-ups that had been cluttering up her psyche for years were coming to the forefront. But—

Miriam's eyes narrowed as she looked inward—that still didn't necessarily mean that Jay *hadn't* been having an affair with Belinda…did it?

She twisted restlessly, the doubt that had crept in unnerving. Imagining she'd got it wrong last Christmas, that what she'd seen was Belinda trying to seduce Jay, that he'd been telling the truth all along and Belinda had lied, was nearly as bad as if it was true, she realised with a stab of horror that she could think that way. But it was. Because that would not only mean she had put them both through the worst year in history for nothing, but also that she'd be back to wondering every minute of every day when the moment would be that Jay would grow tired of her and *really* start an affair with a Belinda lookalike. Because Jay was right. She *had* been waiting for him to let her down as her father had let her mother down.

Miriam groaned softly, her hands cupping her cheeks as she stared blindly ahead. And that feeling was still there, even though she had brought it into the light. She didn't trust him. Awful maybe—especially if he *hadn't* been playing around with Belinda, which perhaps was a possibility—but that was how she felt. In spite of all the pain and loneliness and grief the last ten months, she'd had something—call it peace of mind or a calm acceptance of fate, she wasn't sure, but whatever it was it had been a comfort, even in her worst moments.

The telephone rang, making her jump violently. Becoming aware she was sitting at an empty desk and she had a pile of work to do, she quickly lifted the receiver, her voice clipped and professional when she said, 'Mr Thorpe's secretary. How can I help you?'

'I can think of several ways.' Jay's voice was smokily

amused and her stomach tightened. That was another thing about him, she thought despairingly. He had the most seductive, come-to-bed voice she'd ever heard.

Clearing her throat, she said fairly steadily, 'Jay? What are you doing phoning me at work? Is anything wrong?'

'I'm afraid I can't make it tonight or the next few nights, come to that. A problem's arisen with a business deal and it means making a trip to Germany. Unavoidable.'

'That's all right.' Her main feeling was one of relief. Since the moment he had walked back into her life there hadn't been one day she hadn't seen him and she needed some time to *think*, time that wouldn't be complicated by his presence. She was feeling emotionally claustrophobic, hemmed in. He wouldn't understand that—how could he? She didn't understand herself any more.

'All right?' It was a dry murmur. 'I'd have preferred a smidgen of disappointment.'

'You have to do what your business dictates. I'm aware of that,' she prevaricated.

'An understanding wife.' Now the mockery was overt. 'A rare thing.'

'If you've just phoned to be nasty—'

'I've called to say I'm taking you out to lunch, considering I shan't be around for a few days. I'll be waiting outside at one, OK?'

'I can't. Really, I can't. I didn't get in till a little while ago. Clara wasn't feeling too well and I stayed with her for a couple of hours this morning. I'll work through my lunch hour to catch up.'

'You can work late tonight now you aren't seeing me.'

'There are things that won't wait,' she said firmly, annoyed by his authoritative tone.

'Too true, and one of them is me. One o'clock, Miriam, or I'll come up and get you.'

'You most certainly will not,' she almost hissed at him. 'Who do you think you are anyway?' Stupid question and, Jay being Jay, he didn't miss the opportunity to hammer the point home.

'Your husband?' he drawled silkily. 'Remember? One o'clock sharp.' And the phone went dead.

Great. Just great. Miriam thought about calling him back and then decided against it. There was no point. She had heard the sliver of steel under the silky quality to his voice and it meant he wasn't going to back down.

She glanced at her watch. Half-past eleven and she hadn't so much as switched on her computer or looked through the pile of papers awaiting her attention. What was happening to her? She was beginning to fall apart.

This cheery thought provided a dose of adrenaline. Gritting her teeth, she knuckled down to some work, resolutely banishing Jay from her mind. Or attempting to at least.

A few minutes before one o'clock an inner alarm clock rang, and after glancing at her watch Miriam gathered her coat and handbag together, made a quick visit to the ladies' cloakroom, where she checked her hair and makeup, and then made her way to the foyer of the building. As the lift doors opened she saw Jay immediately. He was sitting in one of the big, plumpy sofas scattered about the reception area, one leg crossed over the other knee and his arms stretched back along the top of the seat. His beautifully tailored suit and silver-gray shirt and tie were of the best quality—naturally—but it was the way they sat on the powerful male body that was breathtaking. And Miriam's breath did catch, literally, along with a flood of pure, unadulterated sexual desire bringing hot colour to her cheeks.

Jay saw her in the next instant, rising to his feet with a lazy smile. 'One minute to go,' he said, his eyes stroking over her face. 'And then I was coming to find you.'

'You wouldn't have,' she protested reprovingly, her flesh tingling as he took her coat from her arm and helped her on with it before reaching for his own black overcoat, which had been slung on the sofa beside him.

'Why not?' Tawny-gold eyes mocked her but his voice held a deep, gritty note when he added, 'It wouldn't be the first time.'

She made no comment to this. In the lift she had made up her mind she would be cool and polite this lunchtime, and once he was back from Germany she'd continue along that line until Christmas, when she would reiterate her demand for a divorce. She didn't want a dramatic finale to all this, tears and recrimination and bitterness. She just wanted to walk away and know some peace again.

You coward, a separate part of her mind said accusingly. It was true what he said, you did run away and you're still running.

Maybe, she answered silently as Jay took her arm, and anguish, hot and sharp, speared her through. But that was better than returning to how she had felt when she had lived with him. She hadn't liked the person she'd become then; jealous, watchful, frightened. So self-preservation dictated this relationship had to end, this *marriage* had to end.

The odd snowflake was still wafting about in the wind as they exited the building and Jay looked up into the leaden grey sky as he said, 'You can smell the snow coming. I wouldn't be surprised if we have a white Christmas.'

How could he mention Christmas so casually? A lump expanded in Miriam's throat. Swallowing hard, she said, 'I have to be back at two o'clock, so it'll have to be a quick lunch.'

'No problem. I've booked a table at a place round the corner as I thought we might be tight on time.'

The place round the corner turned out to be the restaurant of a five-star hotel, where the starters cost as much as a three-course meal anywhere else. They were ushered to a table for two and presented with the menus, and it was then Miriam saw the bottle of champagne nestling in an ice bucket. She raised her eyebrows at Jay, who smiled unrepentantly. 'I'm not driving today and, as we won't be seeing each other for a few days, I thought we'd spoil ourselves. It'll oil the cogs, you'll see. You'll get through twice as much work this afternoon.'

She was too worked up to argue, and as the attentive waiter was already filling their glasses she submitted with good grace, although she never normally drank at lunchtime. It was absolutely delicious, though, a hint of strawberries and summer days present in the sparkling bubbles. By the time the waiter returned to take their order Miriam was shocked to find her glass was empty. It was too drinkable, she decided as the waiter refilled her glass. She wouldn't have any more until she had eaten something.

Once they were alone again, Jay reached across the table and took her cold fingers in his warm hands. 'I shall miss you,' he murmured softly. 'Will you miss me?'

Suddenly she knew she would. Retrieving her fingers under the pretext of fiddling with her linen napkin, which the waiter had placed across her lap after offering her a roll from the basket he'd brought to the table, Miriam smiled coolly. 'You're only going away for a day or two,' she said quietly, busying herself with breaking a morsel from the roll and buttering it.

'That wasn't what I asked.'

Miriam popped the bread in her mouth. He was different today, she thought, but she couldn't put her finger on how. 'I've lots to do for Christmas—cards to write and presents to buy—so I'll be busy.'

'That still wasn't what I asked.'

She stared at him. She loved this man to the core of her being, she thought with frightening intensity. And she wished with all her heart she'd never met him. She had been happy once. Oh, maybe not in the same way she had been happy with Jay; her life had held none of the passion and emotion and sheer joy knowing him had brought. But neither had she experienced the devastation and misery which was the other side of the coin to love.

He was still waiting for an answer. As lightly as she could, she shrugged. 'Of course I'll miss you.'

'You could at least try to pretend you mean that.'

'What do you want me to say, Jay?' she said a trifle sharply, hiding her torment under a veneer of irritation. 'I've told you I'll be busy and it's not as if we live together; I was used to being on my own before we started seeing each other again.'

He poured himself another glass of champagne and for something to do in the awkward silence Miriam found herself drinking hers. When she put her glass down Jay silently reached across and topped it up before settling back in his seat and surveying her with a brooding gaze. 'I want you,' he said quietly, out of the blue. 'Do you want me? Physically, I mean? Or have I got that wrong as well?

Because I'm beginning to think not making love to you over these last weeks wasn't such a bright idea after all.'

All thoughts of being careful went out of the window and she took another fortifying sip of champagne. She needed the buzz. 'What do you mean?' she asked weakly.

'We were good together,' he murmured softly. 'That's what I mean. I want to touch you and taste you and love you.'

Her heart was thudding and she prayed he couldn't see her agitation. She could feel his warmth and sensuality reaching out to her as though he was a magnetic force, drawing her to him whether she wanted it or not. 'We agreed—'

'To hell with what we agreed. Tell me you don't want me and I'll walk away but I don't believe you stopped loving me, in spite of what you thought I'd done. That's true, isn't it? And these last weeks it's been heaven and hell, having you so close and not loving you properly. You've felt it as well, you must have done.'

If he only knew how many endless nights of tossing and turning she'd endured. Miriam cleared her throat. She needed to think; her emotions always took over where Jay was concerned. 'Why—?' Her voice cracked and she tried again. 'Why are you saying this now?'

'Because I'm leaving for a few days and I don't want to go without making love to you,' he said simply. 'Ring in and say you're feeling ill and then come upstairs with me to one of the rooms.'

Miriam shivered. He had planned this when he had invited her to lunch. Instead of anger the thought brought instant excitement. Her throat went dry as a throbbing heat invaded her lower stomach. 'I can't.'

'You can.' The cat-like eyes held hers. 'It's easy, so easy. Come upstairs with me.'

'They—they might not have a room vacant.' She wondered if he'd already reserved one.

It appeared not. 'We'll find out.'

She couldn't. She couldn't skive off work to go to a strange hotel room in the middle of the day to make love. It was, well, faintly immoral. 'But we haven't any luggage and we're not staying overnight,' she whispered tremblingly.

'They don't care. A room's a room and if you pay the going rate for twenty-four hours, it's no skin off their nose.' He leaned towards her, his hand stroking the side of her face. 'Come upstairs with me,' he said again, his voice husky. 'Please, Miriam. I need you so much.'

She needed him. She didn't know whether it was the champagne or just the intoxication of the moment but she was drowning in the flood of desire that was banishing all rational thought. This was crazy, insane, but why shouldn't she step out of time and have this last memory for all the cold, long days and nights to come? She would never love anyone else, she knew that, and so this would have to last a lifetime.

'What—what about our food?' she managed shakily.

Jay grinned. A sexy, enigmatic grin that sent her legs to jelly. 'Is that a yes?'

The feeling of recklessness was heady. She nodded.

'Then I'll take care of it. Wait here.'

She saw him walk across to the head waiter and say something as he extracted his wallet from his jacket, then he was walking back to her, handsome, smiling and superbly confident. For a second the knowledge of what she was going to do intruded into the bubble Jay had induced, but then he had reached her and it was easy to let go of reality and live in the moment.

She stood up and he slid an arm round her waist and together they walked out of the restaurant and into the reception area of the hotel. Jay continued to hold her as he spoke to the receptionist, who was all cool efficiency. The girl didn't bat an eyelid when Jay signed the register as Mr and Mrs Carter, even though Miriam turned a brilliant shade of pink, her embarrassment not helped when Jay requested a bottle of champagne and a large bowl of strawberries be sent up to their suite. In view of the fact they had no luggage the receptionist handed Jay the key to the room and again Miriam had to admire the girl's professionalism. She just wished she could have matched her for coolness. As it was she felt like a scarlet woman as they entered the lift, her cheeks burning. 'She didn't believe we're husband and wife,' she said weakly to Jay as the lift smoothly began to ascend.

He took her in his arms, his fingers tightening in her hair as he tilted her head back and his lips moved over hers. 'Does it matter?'

No, nothing mattered but this moment. And maybe the girl was right anyway. Maybe she was a wanton hussy. Her hands slid up the muscular wall of his chest and caressed the back of his neck, feeling the soft hair at his shirt collar. He smelt divine, that mixture of aftershave and something that was purely Jay. She loved him. She loved him more than life and that was why she couldn't go back to him. It really didn't matter any more whether he had slept with Belinda or not; this wasn't about a particular woman but how she viewed him and women in general. If she went back to him she would end up destroying herself and perhaps him too, if what he had said was the truth and he hadn't been messing around. *But they would have this one afternoon.*

She pressed into him, into the hard evidence of his arousal, parting her lips as he deepened the kiss. And one afternoon would have to do.

CHAPTER EIGHT

THE suite was beautiful. She had been going to protest when Jay had requested that rather than a double room, but in view of what the receptionist must be thinking already she'd let the moment pass. Nevertheless, a suite for just an hour or so was an incredible indulgence, Miriam thought as she stood in the tastefully decorated sitting room. Beyond this, open sliding doors led to a large bedroom. She could just see the enormous bed and floor-length drapes at the window.

She didn't have time to notice anything more before Jay drew her into his arms and kissed her again. It was a soft kiss, a slow kiss, one that was giving her time to respond at her own pace. She hadn't realised she was holding herself so tautly until she began to relax against him, the magic of his mouth working its spell as she floated on a cloud of familiar sexual excitement. Jay had been a generous and experienced lover and she had missed his erotic, sometimes tender, sometimes urgent lovemaking more than she had dreamed possible.

She loved him and she would never stop loving him, no matter what he did. That in itself was terrifying. For a moment she tensed again but she couldn't resist what his mouth and hands were doing to her and suddenly she was hungry for all of him.

She sighed softly as desire flowed like hot melted honey into every part of her, enveloping her in sensual bliss. The first time he had ever kissed her she had wanted the moment to go on forever, amazed that a kiss could be so phenomenally sweet, and once they had married she knew he'd spoiled her for any other man, having awakened her to levels of ecstasy she'd never imagined in her wildest fantasies.

She pressed against his hardness, feeling his shudder of pleasure with fierce satisfaction that she could induce such desire in him. Bending, he scooped her up into his arms and walked through to the bedroom, laying her on the soft quilted bedspread with exquisite gentleness as he murmured endearments against her feverish skin.

He undressed her slowly, savouring each second and admiring her with his eyes, his hands, his mouth until she was stretched out naked in front of him. As she reached out to do the same for him they heard a knock on the outer door. 'The champagne.' Jay smiled at her, kissing her deeply before he said, 'I'll see to it. Pull the covers over yourself if you're cold.'

As he closed the bedroom door behind him Miriam did just that, not because she was chilled—the room was as warm as toast—but with Jay fully clothed she felt suddenly shy. She heard him speak to someone and then the sound of the door closing again before he re-entered the bedroom, pushing a food trolley. It held champagne nestling in an ice bucket, along with two flutes, an enormous bowl of fat red strawberries and a plate of luscious handmade chocolates. 'They think of everything.' He smiled at her as he poured two glasses of champagne and brought them over to the bed, handing her one as he sat down beside her. 'To an afternoon of wicked satisfaction.'

Miriam drank deeply. The brief interlude had brought home the fact she was here, in a hotel room with Jay on a Monday lunchtime when the rest of the world was getting on with the nine-to-five grind. She should feel guilty and ashamed of herself—there were all sorts of things to see to this afternoon. 'I need to phone the office and explain,' she said quickly, knowing once he touched her again coherent thought would go out of the window.

Silently Jay handed her the phone and sipped his champagne as he listened to her explain she wasn't as well as she'd thought and would need the rest of the day off after all to fully recover. As she finished the call he slid off the bed and fetched the bowl of strawberries, throwing himself down beside her and lazily offering her one of the juicy red fruits as he murmured, 'Your medication, ma'am.'

She bit into the luscious sweetness as he held the strawberry to her lips, feeling a little like a femme fatale from the old silent movies. Jay licked a remnant of juice from her lips. 'Delicious.' His tawny eyes were glittering. 'Why haven't we done this before?'

'Spent a fortune on a hotel suite for an hour or two?' she said with an attempt at mockery to hide what being close to him like this was doing to her.

'Stepped out of life and said to hell with the rest of the world.'

'Is that what we're doing?'

'Oh, yes.' He took the empty glass from her hand and placed it on the bedside cabinet before taking her mouth again, kissing her until she was melting. His hands slid beneath the covers, drawing them back and exploring her soft curves until a searing heat flowed through every nerve and sinew.

It felt so good, so right to be this close to him. As she let her senses take over, Miriam wound her arms round his neck, pulling him closer. 'You've still got your clothes on,' she whispered plaintively, needing to be able to touch his bare flesh and feel him, alive and virile beneath her fingertips.

'Undress me.' He brought her hands to the buttons of his shirt. 'I'm yours to command.'

Her hands shook as she undid the tiny buttons but then she was peeling the cloth from his wide shoulders, exulting in the warm, supple skin and muscled strength beneath. Her fingers tangled in the short, soft hair on his chest and she sighed, bending and letting her mouth savour the slightly salty taste of one erect nipple.

She felt the involuntary jerk of pleasure and licked her way across the roughness of his chest to the other nipple, sucking and teasing as he groaned raggedly.

She was aware of him moving back to loosen his belt and then he dragged his thighs free of his trousers, his briefs following a second later along with his shoes and socks. Stark naked, he settled beside her, reaching to enfold her against him as he muttered, 'I don't know how long I can wait, Miriam. It's been a long time…'

She didn't want him to wait. The wantonness was part of the unreality of it all. She wanted him to take her, making her flesh join with his until they were one perfect whole. She needed to feel him inside her, carving a place that was all his own.

As though in response to her thoughts Jay eased her thighs apart, but instead of the quick, urgent coupling she'd expected he began to kiss and taste her with a warm sensuality that brought her to fever-pitch. She writhed and arched as pleasure became unbearable in its intensity and she moaned in pure ecstasy. His lovemaking was as mind-blowing as it had always been but somehow different. Or perhaps *she* was different, she thought with a stab of reason, now she had stopped fooling herself and pretending this was for ever. Knowing this was the last time they would be together like this made it bitter-sweet and infinitely precious.

'You're beautiful, do you know that? Inside and out, you're beautiful,' he whispered huskily as he raised his head to look at her flushed face.

'I'm not beautiful,' she murmured shakily. Not like some of those other women he had dated.

'You're so beautiful you take my breath away.' His lips claimed hers, urgent and searching, and she gave herself up to the desire that was making her tremble uncontrollably.

When he finally entered her he filled her completely, devouring her with the need to make her his. And she met him thrust for thrust, wanting to give him pleasure as he was pleasuring her. They moved together in a rhythm as ancient as time but still Jay paced himself, building the intensity of their shared passion until she thought she would explode in a million pieces. The crescendo of sexual need for release increased, her internal muscles contracting to a point where she was stunned by the savagery of what she was experiencing. It was pain and pleasure and exquisite torment, their long months apart heightening every movement.

Her body tightened as she reached her peak and at the same moment she felt Jay's response, their climax violent in its wild fulfillment. She drew in sobbing gasps of air, his name on her lips as their two bodies blended as one.

She couldn't stop trembling in the aftermath of their passion but Jay's body was shaking too as he drew her closer against him, kissing her lips, her closed eyelids, her forehead. 'So many nights I've dreamt of this,' he murmured softly as her body slowly quietened, 'wondering if you were awake too, what you were thinking, whether I featured in your thoughts or dreams. I'd smell the scent of you, hear you whisper my name... I thought I was going crazy...'

She curled into him, settling herself more comfortably in the circle of his arms. She was gloriously, achingly, satisfyingly tired, content to drift into the warm haven of his closeness without the real world intruding. She kissed the warm skin at the base of his throat, inhaling the scent of him. 'You smell the same,' she murmured throatily.

'Is that good?'

'Oh, yes.' Miriam raised her head slightly and he took her mouth in answer to the silent request, kissing her gently until she pressed her body against his arousal. By the time he moved his body over hers again she was ready to receive him, the slow sensuality of his lovemaking achingly tender. As she felt him inside her she moaned softly, relishing the feelings he evoked and the way the need to please her always came first with him. He had always been the same in that regard but she knew from listening to the other women at work talking amongst themselves that not all men were so considerate.

Their joining became more intense and passionate, an exquisite physical pleasure taking her into a world of sensation and light where nothing mattered but Jay and what he was doing to her. She wouldn't think beyond this stolen afternoon. Not now. Time enough for that later.

They stayed in bed all afternoon, making love, eating the strawberries and chocolates and finishing off the champagne. Outside the hotel window the sky drew dark with snow and then big fat flakes began to fall, whirling and dancing against the glass. At some point Miriam had pulled back the curtains so she could watch the storm and she knew she would never forget this day; Jay's arms about her, the warmth of his flesh against hers, the cosiness of their hideaway and the taste of their shared passion on her tongue.

They didn't talk about their yesterdays or their tomorrows, they didn't talk much at all and when they did it was mostly soft murmurings and lazy nothings. They simply existed in each precious minute as it ticked by.

It was nearly five o'clock and completely dark outside when Jay nudged the top of her head with his chin, whispering softly, 'I have to go. I don't want to—hell, that's the understatement of the year, but I've got a plane to catch.'

Miriam had been lying curled into him, her fingers stroking the supple, smooth skin of his back and her cheek buried against the hair on his chest. She closed her eyes tightly for one moment and then opened them to move slightly and gaze up at him. 'I know.'

He kissed her hungrily. 'I don't want to leave you but there's a lot hanging on my sorting things out in Germany, not least men's jobs.'

'It's all right, really.' She forced a smile. 'I know you have to go, Jay. It's not a problem.'

He smiled, kissing her once more before sitting up, one hand lingering on her silky flesh for a second. Then he swung his feet off the bed and padded across to the *en suite*. 'I'll shower quickly,' he said over his shoulder. 'Would you mind having a cup of coffee waiting for me? Black, please.'

Miriam pulled on one of the thick white robes which had been waiting for them in the suite and busied herself making the coffee from the complimentary tray in the sitting room. When Jay joined her he was already dressed, his black hair damp from the shower. He walked across to where she was sitting, touching the side of her face with a tender hand as he said, 'I love you so much. You know that, don't you?'

She nodded before saying the words he had a right to hear. 'I love you too.'

His breath caught at her declaration and he pulled her to her feet, holding her loosely within the circle of his arms as he murmured, 'Does that mean what I want it to mean?'

She had known this moment would come, of course. All afternoon she had known it at the back of her mind and it had made each moment all the more bitter-sweet. She didn't try to prevaricate or play dumb. Lowering her eyes because she couldn't bear to look at his face while she said it, she said equally softly, 'I can't be what you need, Jay.'

'I need *you*. That's all. Just you as you are.'

'No.' She pulled away and he let her go, the tawny eyes tight on her face. 'You need someone who can enjoy being part of your world and take what it means to be your wife in her stride; the social functions, the dinner parties, the entertaining, the—the women.'

'I didn't have an affair with Belinda,' he said quietly. 'From the first moment we met there has been no one but you.'

Funnily enough, for the first time she believed him. 'That doesn't make any difference.'

'Doesn't make any difference?' He stared at her. 'What the hell are you talking about? You left me because you believed I had been having some sort of relationship with that woman and after the lies she told and the way you found us at the office that night I couldn't blame you for thinking the worst initially. I hoped reason would kick in and tell you I couldn't possibly have betrayed you like that when you'd had a chance to think about it, I admit, but I hadn't allowed for how deep the damage over what your father did to your mother had gone. But I love you, Miriam. You love me. What are we fighting about?'

'We're not fighting.'

'I want you as my wife. *You*. No one else.'

Nothing he was saying was making her feel any better. Something had broken in her that afternoon. The problem wasn't Jay, it was her, and she would always be this way. She knew she would. And she didn't want to ruin both their lives with her jealousy and distrust and turn Jay into someone he wasn't. Shaking her head slowly, she murmured, 'Remember the good times, remember this afternoon; let it end like this.'

'The hell I will.' His eyes glittered like spun gold in the subdued lighting in the sitting room. 'This is not some play or film, Miriam. We're real people in a real situation without a dramatic fade-out, and if agreeing to spend the afternoon with me was your idea of a swansong then you can forget it. I'm not got rid of so easily.'

'You don't understand.'

'You're dead right there.'

She didn't think she had ever seen him so angry. 'It's me, not you,' she said wearily. 'At first I thought you *had* been seeing Belinda but over the last weeks I faced the fact that might not be true and I'd made a terrible mistake.'

'It wasn't and you did,' he put in grimly.

'But there'll be other Belindas, don't you see?' she said jaggedly. 'Women *like* you; they throw themselves at you.'

He stated the obvious. 'I can't help that.'

'I know that. I know you don't encourage them but it happens anyway. Another woman might be able to take that in her stride but I can't. I know that now. I—I should never have agreed to marry you, Jay. It was a disaster waiting to happen.'

Red streaks of temper were searing colour across his cheekbones but his voice was more controlled, low and steady, when he said, 'This is nonsense. Are you seriously telling me that you accept there was never anything going on with Belinda, or anyone else if it comes to it, but it doesn't make any difference to the way you feel about ending our marriage? That doesn't make sense and you know it. I've told you how I feel about you; what more do you want from me?'

Struggling for calmness, she said, 'If I came back to you we'd end up hating each other eventually. Jealousy does that. I—I love you but I can't trust you. I can't, Jay. I've tried but all the time at the back of my mind I'd be questioning, wondering when the one is going to appear who *would* get your attention.'

'I've told you, she's here.'

'And I believe you. At this moment.' There was a tinge of panic to her voice as she tried to make him understand. 'But outside these four walls is the world and we have to live in it. That's where I'd fail. That's where I'd fail *you*.'

'I'm not accepting that.'

'You have to.'

'What can I say to convince you?'

'You can't.'

'Damn it, Miriam, have the courage to put the past behind you.' He was breathing hard in the effort to hold on to his temper. 'I'm not your father any more than you're your mother. We're two different people with a different life together. I can't alter who I am, the way I look, and I wouldn't if I could. I'm me. I'm not ashamed of it. I was always absolutely honest with you about my past relationships. I sowed my wild oats, we both know that, but I never told a woman I loved her until I met you and I sure as hell never asked one to marry me. When I met you I fell head over heels, you know that too. I told you it's the kind of love that will last for ever, that I wanted you to be the mother of my children, that I wanted the roses round the door and commitment and the whole caboodle, and nothing's changed. Not for me.'

She had to do this. It was tearing her apart but it would be worse in the future if she gave in now. Somehow she had to make him *see*. Trying to find the words to explain the truth of how it was, she said, 'I know and, like I said, this is my fault, not yours. I love you, although you might not believe it, but that itself is the problem. If—if I didn't love you so much I wouldn't feel this way but the whole time we were married I was on edge. I didn't realise it until that night I saw you with Belinda but it's the truth. And I don't want to live like that, Jay.'

'So you're telling me you love me but you don't trust me or want to remain married to me?' he said in a low, tight voice. 'Then forgive me but your idea of love stinks. Don't you think I get jealous too? That I've been burnt up with it since you left, wondering if some other guy would sweet-talk you into believing you'd be better off with him while you're in such a vulnerable state? Times I wanted to come and get you, drag you back by force if necessary, but I didn't because I genuinely believed you needed time to come to terms with this stuff. I was foolish enough to trust in *you*, in your love for me, all the promises and the vows we made on the day we married. And now you're telling me you want to throw away what we had, what we still have, because you're too damn cowardly to come out of the past and live in the present?'

He was breathing hard, his eyes angry and hostile. Miriam felt paralysed by the force of his rage. She tried to think of something to say and failed utterly. She *was* a coward, she thought wretchedly. And his opinion of her couldn't be lower than the one she had of herself. But it didn't change her mind. 'I'm sorry,' she said again, weakly.

'No you're not.' His words were emphasised by the silence that followed, a silence that pressed on the nerve-endings until it was a force in itself, dark and angry. After some long moments he ground out, 'If you were sorry that would be something to work with but you're so damn sure you're right about all this. You're content to retreat into yourself and lock the door in your mind labelled love and throw away the key, that's it at bottom. You've always faintly despised your mother for loving your father the way she did, but I tell you this. If you had half her backbone and courage you'd be doing all right.'

'How dare you?' Suddenly the weakness was gone and she was furiously, blazingly angry. 'I have never despised my mother, not for one second. Just because I didn't agree with her wasting years of her life waiting for a man who wasn't worthy to lick her boots, it didn't mean I thought any the less of her.'

'If you didn't despise her it frightened you though, didn't it?' he said more quietly. 'Terrified you. Tied you up in knots.'

His insight was more unnerving than his rage. Bracing herself, she said tightly, 'Haven't you a plane to catch?'

'That's it? Don't tell me, you aren't prepared to discuss this any further, right? Because I'm getting close, too close.'

She went for total honesty. 'Yes, you are. And I can't handle that, OK? More than that, I don't *want* to handle it. I should never have married you, Jay. I'm not cut out for marriage. I see that now.'

'Rubbish.' Eyes that had turned as hard as amber held hers. 'Like you've pointed out so distinctly, I come into contact with a lot of women and you're more suited to be a wife and mother than all of them. Look at this after-noon—can you tell me in all truthfulness it wasn't heaven on earth? We didn't have sex, Miriam. We made love. There's a hell of a difference.'

She steeled herself to remain strong. 'This afternoon was—was goodbye.'

'You don't mean that.'

She raised her head and no one could have mistaken the determination in her voice. 'Yes, I do,' she said.

The moment stretched and lengthened. 'Goodbye?' he said softly. 'You're sure about that?'

He reached out and stroked a wisp of hair from her face, his fingers lingering on the silky skin of her neck. Miriam fought the unbidden visceral response to his touch with all her might. Somehow she managed to keep the trembling out of her voice as she said, 'Yes, I'm sure. When you come back from Germany I don't think we should see each other. There—there's no point. You must see that? It's just prolonging the agony.'

'The arrangement was till Christmas.' The hard, hand-some face was suddenly imperturbable and she couldn't tell what he was thinking. 'Or is that another promise you're going to break?'

'Don't—don't be like this.'

'I rather think that's my line.' He reached down and took the coffee she'd prepared for him, swilling it down in a couple of long gulps before straightening. 'There'll be a taxi waiting downstairs whenever you're ready to leave, but don't rush,' he said evenly, his tone almost completely devoid of expression. 'Goodbye, Miriam.'

His mouth skimmed hers in the lightest of kisses and then he turned before she could speak or react, walking to the door of the suite and opening it.

'Jay?'

Her voice caught him on the threshold and he turned, looking straight into her drowning eyes as he drawled, 'Yes?'

'If you love me like you say you do then please let this be goodbye right now. What's the point in delaying things a couple of weeks?' she said unsteadily. 'I need things to be like they were before we saw each other again.'

She saw him draw a deep breath. 'Then you're crying for the moon,' he said simply.

And shut the door.

CHAPTER NINE

WHEN Miriam left the hotel thirty minutes later the snow which had looked so Christmassy and pretty when she'd been warmly wrapped in Jay's arms in the suite was positively vicious in the wind, stinging her cheeks and whitening her coat before she reached the taxi parked a few yards away.

'We're in for a packet,' the taxi driver remarked cheerfully as she climbed into the back of the cab. 'Can't see much evidence of global warming in this lot, can you? Where to, love?'

After giving him the address, Miriam settled back in her seat and prayed he wouldn't be the chatty sort. The thought of having to make conversation horrified her. As it was the atrocious weather conditions kept him occupied and she was left to her own thoughts, a dubious blessing in the circumstances.

She had made an awful mistake in sleeping with Jay again. How could she have been so foolish? It hadn't been fair on him, sending mixed messages and confusing the issue, and as for her... She bit her lip, trying hard not to cry as she gazed out of the window at the solid sheet of whirling snow. How could she get through the rest of her life without him?

But she would. She blinked the tears away, wishing she were home in her little bedsit with the door locked so she could give way to the storm within. She had been incredibly stupid today to give in to the desire to be close to him one last time but it was done now and she couldn't undo it. She just had to pick herself up and brush herself down and go on from here. Easy—in theory. In practice it might be a whole lot more difficult.

The taxi driver had to drop her at the top of her street because the snow was so thick in the side-roads. As she entered the house she glanced towards Clara's front door and wondered if her friend was in and whether Brian was with her. She hadn't given Clara a thought all afternoon. She stood for a moment or two looking at the closed door. She didn't really want to talk to Clara—she didn't want to talk to *anyone*—but would Clara expect her to ask how things went with Brian? But then if he *was* there they might be otherwise engaged. From the look on both their faces when she'd left that morning she had the feeling the celibacy notion might well have gone out of the window.

Her forehead knit, she stood hesitating and then decided she'd see Clara the next morning before they had to leave for work. By then she would be able to give Clara every ounce of her attention without being worried she was going to spoil the moment by crying all over her.

Once in her bedsit Miriam drew the curtains to shut the world out and took off her coat and shoes. Her feet were icy cold and damp where she'd waded through the thick snow to reach the house, and she decided she'd change and pop down the landing to the bathroom for a long, hot soak.

But still she just sat there on her sofa, feeling waves of self-recrimination wash over her. She was stupid, so stupid. And what must Jay be thinking? He'd obviously assumed everything had been sorted between them when she'd spent the whole afternoon making love, and why wouldn't he?

He had been so angry. She groaned, her eyes liquid with tears. The things he had said... Not that she blamed him for any of it—in fact, how could she when he was absolutely right? But it had still been painful to hear.

She swallowed hard, telling herself she had to get it together, and then her mobile rang. Reaching for her bag, she got her phone out, half expecting it to be her mother, in which case she'd let the answer machine cut in. But the little screen said otherwise.

Her voice shaking, she said, 'Hello, Jay.'

'I'm at the airport,' he said flatly, 'but I wanted to make sure you got home OK. You are home, I take it?'

She nodded and then realised what she was doing. She was definitely losing it. 'Yes, I'm home.'

'Good. The weather's foul and we're grounded as we speak but apparently there are signs the storm'll be over shortly.' There was a pause and Miriam wondered if he expected her to say something, but she couldn't. He might detect her silent tears.

'Look, Miriam, I've been thinking over what you said, about not seeing each other when I'm back from this trip. After all we said this afternoon I'm beginning to see there's no hope for us. To be frank I don't think I can take any more of this banging my head against a brick wall.' He paused again, and then said, 'Miriam? Are you there?'

It took more willpower than she'd imagined she possessed to keep the tears out of her voice when she said, 'I'm here.'

'You clearly want out.'

'Yes.'

'And your mind's made up.'

'Yes.'

'Then perhaps it's better if we do this quickly and cleanly right now without any long-drawn-out goodbyes or bad feeling. What do you say?'

Somehow she managed the one word again. 'Yes.' He might think she was being awkward but he'd never know the effort it was taking to get that solitary word past the enormous constriction that had her throat in a vice.

'OK.' His voice was still flat, almost stony. 'Well, take care of yourself for me. We'll start the ball rolling in the New Year once Christmas is out of the way if that suits? Goodbye, Miriam.'

'Goodbye.' He meant it, she thought sickly. She had got what she wanted, but still when the phone went dead she could hardly believe it had finally ended.

She sat for a long time without moving, senses and mind numb. Aeons later she made herself rise and take off her clothes, slipping on her bathrobe and collecting her toiletries before making her way to the bathroom.

All the while she lay in the hot bubbles the numbness didn't lift and Miriam welcomed it, embraced it. She didn't want to feel, to think. She wanted to stay in this peculiar state of suspended animation for ever.

Eventually, when the water was cool and her skin resembled a wrinkled prune, she made herself get out of the bath and towelled herself dry. After her customary routine of creaming and moisturising she went back to the bedsit and put on her comfortable old pyjamas that had seen better days but which were perfect for couch-potato moments.

She even made herself a plateful of hot buttered toast and a milky hot chocolate, eating her tea curled up on the sofa while she watched the news and then listened to the weather girl—who was muffled up like an Eskimo, having been banished outside to give the forecast as though everyone in Britain didn't know they were in the grip of wintry blizzards—explain this high and that low had caused Siberian storms to hit the UK.

It was just nine o'clock when Clara knocked on the door. Miriam had been watching a comedy-drama but the moment she turned away from the TV she'd forgotten what it was about.

Clara had been grinning like a Cheshire cat when Miriam opened the door. Her face straightening in the blink of an eye, she said, 'What's the matter?'

Miriam wanted to say that nothing was the matter, that everything was fine. She wanted to ask what had happened between Clara and Brian, to say she so hoped everything was sorted out, that Brian seemed a lovely man and she could see the two of them being ecstatically happy together. Instead she stared into her friend's concerned blue eyes and burst into tears.

It was some minutes and plenty of tissues later be-fore Miriam could explain what had happened, and when she did Clara offered no well-meaning advice but simply sat and listened as she patted her hand. Then she made them both a cup of strong coffee and settled herself on the floor at Miriam's feet.

'Let me get this straight.' She tilted her head as she surveyed Miriam's ravaged face. 'You love him and he loves you. You now think he almost certainly *wasn't* carrying on with this awful Poppins woman—'

'He wasn't, I'm sure of it.'

'But you still don't think you can go back to him,' Clara continued as though she hadn't interrupted, 'because…'

'I'd always be waiting for a real Belinda to come along.'

It didn't make sense but Clara understood anyway. 'But if he loves you like he says he does, he wouldn't stray.'

'My father said he loved my mother—he swept her off her feet, in fact. She thought the world revolved around him and when he left her she never really recovered. I…I don't want to be like that, Clara.'

Clara was silent for some thirty seconds, a long time for Clara. Springing up, she fetched the biscuit barrel from the kitchen area and dug out a chocolate digestive. Her mouth full of biscuit, she mumbled, 'I know I've only met your mother once, and that wasn't exactly the hit of the century, but she didn't strike me as the sort of woman to wait forever for a low life like your father.'

Miriam delved in the barrel. 'Well, she did.'

'Are you sure? I mean, have you ever discussed how she felt with her?'

'I didn't have to; I was there, remember?'

'You were a child.' Clara reached for another digestive. 'People see things differently as a child.'

Miriam shrugged. 'I know how it was, Clara.' Purposely changing the subject, she said, 'I didn't like to call on you earlier in case Brian was there. How did things go?'

Clara said, almost apologetically, 'Great, thanks.'

'Hey, just because Jay and I have got problems it doesn't mean I'm not thrilled for you and I want to hear every detail, all right? I mean it. Start at the beginning when you let him in.'

Clara started at the beginning and finished at the end

and by the time she left it was close on midnight. Once snuggled down in bed, however, Miriam found she couldn't sleep. Now her mind had fully emerged from the numb state of shock she found she couldn't turn her thoughts off and they all featured Jay. His golden eyes, his sexy smile, the strong planes and angles of his handsome face, and his body...the broad expanse of hair-roughened chest, his lean muscled stomach, sinewy limbs and powerful arousal. She shivered. She could almost smell the scent of him on her skin, the places where Jay had kissed and caressed and nibbled.

At three o'clock she gave up all thoughts of sleep and after wrapping the duvet around her went and sat by the window. It had stopped snowing and the night was clear and sparklingly new, the rooftops virgin white and the odd light or two in the distance giving a Christmas-card magic to the view.

She'd thought she was all cried out but the lump in her throat indicated otherwise. Jay was probably in Germany now, in some hotel room fast asleep before an early start in the morning. She had always relished the moments she could look at him to her heart's content when he was asleep. He had always appeared more boyish then, his thick eyelashes curling onto his cheekbones and his firm, faintly stern mouth relaxed. But very masculine. And beautiful. Virile. Dangerous.

She made a sound deep in her throat, a hundred and one conflicting emotions tearing at her. She was a mess, she acknowledged bitterly. And she didn't know how to begin to unravel the tangle in her mind.

Gradually the peace and tranquility of the scene outside worked like a soothing balm on her overwrought nerves, her eyelids becoming heavy. She must have dozed for a while, sitting upright cocooned in the duvet, because suddenly it was six in the morning and she knew exactly what she was going to do. Something Clara had said had obviously permeated her subconscious while she slept. She needed to go and see her mother and ask her about her father.

Extracting herself from the duvet, she made a pot of tea, returning to her tiny table and chairs and drinking three cups, looking out at the pink-tinted sky where the first rays of dawn were breaking through. Soon the whole expanse was streaked with faint dusky pink, mother-of-pearl and deep charcoal, the white world beneath reflecting light.

She didn't really know what good it would do to talk to her mother, Miriam reflected as she washed up the tea things, or even if her mother would want to discuss the man who had hurt her so badly. But she had to try. And it would have to be when George was at work.

She phoned her mother at eight o'clock once she was washed and dressed and had put the bedsit to rights.

'Hello, darling.' Anne's voice reflected pleasure at the unexpected call, which made Miriam feel immediately guilty. 'I was only saying to George last night I hadn't heard from you for a day or two.'

More than a day or two. Miriam took the gentle rebuke without commenting. Instead she said, 'I thought I might call and see you this morning if you're not doing anything? We could have lunch somewhere.'

'You're not at work?'

'No.'

'You're ill?'

'I haven't been feeling too good for a couple of days.' That was at least the truth. She had never felt so hopelessly bereft and miserable in her life.

'I'll come to you and bring lunch if you're feeling poorly.'

The thought of her mother sitting in the bedsit and inwardly criticising it every moment was too much. Even when Anne wasn't verbalising comparisons with Jay's luxurious apartment, her face said plenty. 'No, it would do me good to get out. I'll come about eleven if that's OK and we can have coffee first.'

Her mother's 'All right' was reluctant.

Two minutes later the mobile rang, just after Miriam had finished the call to her boss to tell him she needed another day off. Her conscience had led her to confess the problem was a 'domestic difficulty' rather than physical illness and she would be happy to take the two days as holiday entitlement if he wished. He'd told her not to be so silly, wished her well and said he'd see her the following day.

'Miriam?' Her mother's voice was tight. 'I have to ask. This not feeling too good. You aren't coming to tell me you're seriously ill, are you?'

Oh, dear, Miriam thought ruefully. 'No, no. I promise.'

'Cross your heart and hope to die?'

Sometimes Miriam wondered who was the parent and who was the child. 'Absolutely. I'll see you at eleven.'

The small bungalow her mother and George had bought when they had got married was situated on the northern outskirts of London. Miriam took the tube as far as she could and then finished the journey by taxi. The salting lorries had been out the night before and most of the main roads were relatively clear of snow, but the quieter residential areas were a foot deep in places. Her mother's street was no exception but clearly the neighbours had all banded together and the taxi could get almost to her mother's door.

Her mother opened the door before she knocked.

Obviously she'd been looking out for her. They hugged and her mother took her coat and scarf and drew Miriam into the warmth of the kitchen, where the coffee pot was gurgling. Once they were sitting at the kitchen table with a mug of steaming coffee and a piece of fruit cake in front of them, her mother said, 'Well?'

Miriam eyed her mother over the rim of her mug. 'What?'

'Something's the matter.'

'Why should anything be the matter?'

Anne Brown fixed her daughter with a maternal glare. 'This is your mother you're talking to; you can't pull the wool over my eyes. Is it something to do with Jay? You've started the divorce?'

'Not yet.'

'What, then?' And before Miriam could answer: 'Have you seen Jay? You have, haven't you?'

Miriam ran a weary hand through her hair. It would be far easier to come clean in view of what she needed to ask her. 'Mum, I need to talk to you, and just listen for a while, will you? Without interrupting or asking any questions?'

'Darling, I'm a wonderful listener. All my friends say so.'

It took Miriam ten minutes to say what she wanted to say and, much to her amazement, her mother didn't say a word, not even when she related the conversation with Jay word for word, or as closely as she could remember it.

A silence fell as she finished speaking and it stretched for some time before Anne said softly, 'I never dreamt you thought I felt like that about your father.'

Miriam stared at her mother, seeing the too bright eyes with a rush of remorse. 'Oh, don't cry. Mum, don't cry. I didn't want to upset you. If it's still too painful to talk about him, I understand.'

'That's just it. You clearly don't and it's all my fault. Sweetheart, even before you were born I was beginning to think I'd made a terrible mistake in marrying your father, and as for loving him in the years after he'd left us... I hated him. I hated him so much at first I suppose I was frightened of putting my feelings onto you, and after all he *was* your father. I'd seen friends who had been in a similar situation and transferred their bitterness to the children and it did untold damage. I didn't want that for you. So I was careful about what I said and you didn't ask any questions; in fact, you seemed to adjust overnight to him going.'

Miriam blinked, feeling disoriented. 'But you never showed an interest in anyone else; you never dated.'

'I was holding down a full-time job and raising you— that was more than enough in the early years and I didn't want a third party coming in and spoiling our closeness. With such an excuse for a father I felt you deserved every bit of me for a few years, and we had some good times, didn't we?'

'You know we did.' Money might have been tight but her mother had always made sure they did lots together that didn't cost much; picnics, walks in the park, curling up on a winter's evening and playing board games. They'd saved tokens for free visits to museums and art galleries, and had days window shopping when they'd finish their excursion with a milkshake and a burger. She could still remember the thrill she'd got on those outings.

'I was so angry he never tried to find out how you were, never even sent you a birthday card, things like that.' Anne paused. 'But you didn't mention him and so it seemed a good idea to let sleeping dogs lie. I really wasn't bothered about another relationship; I had all I wanted in you. And then George came along at just the right time, when you were growing independent, and it seemed right.'

Miriam was feeling strange; she couldn't believe her version of the past was so at odds with what her mother was saying. She had been angry most of her life that her mother had wasted years loving a man who wasn't worthy of her and it turned out she hadn't loved him at all. Moreover, her mother had *chosen* not to date and remain single because of her. 'There must have been times you resented being left with a child when you were so young.'

'I resented your father absolving himself of all responsibility and disappearing into the blue yonder, but never, for a second, did I regret having you,' her mother said very softly. 'Actually it was the fact he had given me you, the most precious thing in the world, that enabled me to see eventually I didn't hate him after all. How could I? If I hadn't met him I wouldn't have you. But as for loving him... Oh, Miriam. Not in a million years. I fell madly in love with a charming, handsome young man who swept me off my feet and my head was full of visions of orange blossom and a white dress. We married six weeks after we met and within six months I knew him for the shallow, selfish, vain individual he was. But by then I was pregnant and from the second I knew you were on the way I loved you with a consuming love. It didn't seem too much of a hardship to stay with him if it meant my child grew up with two parents.'

'We—we should have talked about this before.' Miriam's voice was faint but she felt heady. She knew she had to get a grasp on this complete turnaround but as yet it wasn't registering.

'Yes, darling, we should, and it's my fault we haven't.

I suppose I thought you were so together, so well-adjusted, there was no need.'

'And I didn't say anything because I didn't want to rake up the past and hurt you.' Miriam took several big gulps of her coffee—she needed the caffeine. 'But it was only after he died that you married George.'

'Yes, I suppose it was but, like I said, I met your stepfather at just the right time. Probably if I had met him earlier I might have been tempted, though, because—and I know this might sound odd coming from your mother with me being the age I am—he's the love of my life, Miriam. And every day I've known him it gets better and better.'

Miriam stared at her mother. Anne's face showed the natural wrinkles and lines of age but it radiated happiness. It had done ever since the day she had met George. Why hadn't she noticed this before? Her stepfather wasn't second-best, not for a minute. 'Jay said you've got a lot of backbone and courage,' she said abruptly.

'Did he?' Anne smiled. 'Bless him. He loves you, you know. Always has, always will. Like George loves me. Jay's as far removed from your father as chalk is from cheese. I don't believe for a minute he did anything with that awful woman and I never will. I know you don't like me to say it but I can't help it, not when so much is at stake.'

Miriam began to cry. Anne set her coffee cup down and knelt in front of her daughter, taking Miriam's hands in her own and shaking them gently. 'Ring him,' she urged. 'Or at least see him when he gets back. Tell him you believe in him.'

'But do I trust him? Like you trust George and women should trust the man they're with? I love him so much it scares me.' Miriam sniffed. 'I'm not brave like you.'

'Oh, yes, you are.' Anne held one of Miriam's hands against her cheek for a moment. 'Believe me, I know.'

'I want to believe it too but I'm not sure, that's the truth of it. And I need to be sure.' Miriam shook her head, her eyes downcast. 'Besides which, I think Jay's had enough. And you don't know him like I do. Once he's made up his mind about something there's no going back. No second thoughts. That's the sort of man he is.'

'He made up his mind he wanted to marry you,' Anne pointed out gently. 'Doesn't that count for anything?' She stood up, hugging Miriam briefly before she said, 'Coffee's all very well but for the very important moments in life there's nothing like a really robust red. I'm going to open a bottle and we'll have lunch here; I've got a couple of steaks and salad and a wicked chocolate mousse waiting to be eaten. How does that sound?'

'It was your and George's dinner,' Miriam guessed.

'George would love to take me out tonight instead—he's always suggesting we eat out more.' Anne hugged her again. 'And don't beat yourself up too badly, sweetheart. You've got quite a bit to come to terms with; don't rush it. If Jay is half the man I think he is, he'll wait. He loves you.'

CHAPTER TEN

MIRIAM often brought her mother's words to mind over the next couple of weeks.

She had been in a state of feverish anticipation when Jay was due to return to the UK, part of her hoping he would contact her and demand they meet, the other part knowing she was still no nearer to being able to say to him that she trusted him absolutely. And with things having gone this far, she knew nothing else would do for Jay.

As it was, the deadline she had set for herself came and went, along with the atrocious weather. With the mercurial ability of the English climate the second week of December was unseasonably mild, the blizzards of the first week a distant memory. If it wasn't for the fact that all the trees were bare and the calendar stated they were in December, folk could have been forgiven for thinking it was early October.

And Jay didn't call.

Miriam shopped with Clara for the clothes and accessories they needed for their Christmas break, wrote endless Christmas cards and made sure any gifts were taken care of by way of seasonal hampers being delivered. She couldn't face being in the midst of harassed Christmas shoppers this year. Pathetic, she knew, but with every minute that passed with no contact from Jay she just wanted Christmas to be over. In fact she was wondering why she had ever thought the season was such a great time.

Her mother was—amazingly—incredibly tactful in the midst of it all. She didn't ask after Jay once, although she must have been dying to know what was happening, and was positively encouraging about Miriam's skiing holiday with Clara. Because this reeked of maternal pity it didn't particularly hearten Miriam, but it did take a bit of the heat off. Especially regarding Great-Aunt Abigail.

Three days before Christmas Eve it began to get markedly colder. Colleagues at work who were normally cynical and cool talked excitedly of a white Christmas and every time Miriam turned the radio or TV on the latest pop song—'Christmas Every Day of the Year'—seemed to burst forth. Even the worldly-wise Clara was infected with the festive bug, or maybe it was just her relationship with Brian, which was going from strength to strength, that had Clara humming carols and buying a tree for the lobby of the house. Miriam helped her friend decorate it with tinsel and baubles, laughing her first genuine laugh for days when instead of a fairy for the top of the tree Clara produced a somewhat scary-looking scarecrow complete with red Father Christmas hat.

'Can't be too traditional, now, can I?' Clara grinned. 'Got my reputation to think of. Cool, eh?'

'Dead cool,' Miriam agreed affectionately. 'Although why you've gone to all this trouble when we aren't going to be around for Christmas, I don't know.' They were due to leave early morning on Christmas Eve and be away for nine days.

Clara reeled off the names of the other occupants of the

house. 'They'll enjoy it,' she said, a holy glow of magnanimity surrounding her. 'It is the season of goodwill to man after all.'

'True.' Miriam smiled as she looked at the sweet-smelling tree with its ridiculous topknot but her heart was aching. It was getting worse, not better, this gnawing yearning for Jay. The heaviness in her spirit was weighing her down, making everything an effort, the more so because she was now questioning how he could have cut her out of his life so completely if he loved her as he said he did.

It was unreasonable, she told herself sternly. Totally unreasonable in view of all she'd said to him. She was the one who had sent Jay away, who'd insisted there was no hope for them, so why would the poor man attempt to see her again? She was asking too much. Probably she had always asked too much of him and with women throwing themselves at his feet Jay didn't have to put up with a nutcase who had all manner of hang-ups cluttering up her psyche. No, she couldn't in all honesty blame Jay for deciding enough was enough and moving on.

But she did.

She could always pick up the phone and call him. This was another thing she told herself constantly, but somehow, in spite of now knowing she had been wrong about her mother all those years, the thought of laying herself wide open was beyond her. Which probably meant she still had some gremlins to get rid of, she admitted miserably. No, not probably. Absolutely definitely. And so the endless soul-searching continued.

The day before Christmas Eve saw the first light snowfall, just enough to provide a frosting on the bare trees and rooftops and send already excited children into a frenzy of anticipation. As it was the office Christmas party in the afternoon little work was done, the firm winding down for a Christmas break which extended to the day after New Year's Day.

Miriam had a couple of glasses of wine and some nibbles, joining in the chatter and laughter and pretending an excitement about her holiday she didn't feel for the sake of social intercourse. She had been doing the same with Clara for the last couple of weeks, not wishing to spoil her friend's anticipation just because of how she was feeling.

By the time she left the centrally heated confines of the building for the London streets it was bitterly cold and the smell of frost was in the air. The pavements were crowded with Christmas shoppers carrying laden bags and parcels, everyone intent on their own business and seemingly devoid of any Christmas spirit if the pushing and shoving was anything to go by.

She'd had her fill of city life. As the thought hit, Miriam realised it was in the form of a revelation. She'd had years of living and working in the metropolis and it had been great at first, stimulating and exhilarating, even if her job was fairly predictable. But did she really want to fight her way through a stream of people every morning and again at night for the rest of her life whilst living in a concrete jungle?

A harassed mother with a toddler hanging on to the side of the pushchair and a snotty-nosed baby crying its head off passed her, the woman's shopping bag bumping into her with enough force to cause her to stumble. The woman marched on as Miriam looked, barging her way through the crowd as she used the pushchair almost as a weapon to clear the way in front of her.

But this was Jay's world. This was where he functioned,

where he wanted to be, right in the heart of the pulsing city. His apartment was proof of that. And there was nothing wrong with his choice; it wasn't bad. But it wasn't what she wanted any more.

The thought was incredibly disturbing but one she realised she had been coming to for a long time, probably from the first day they had split. Loving him as she did, she had fitted into the hectic social whirl of dinner parties and entertaining, and to be fair she had enjoyed it some of the time. But now, although she didn't want to live as a hermit, she needed something different. Grass, trees, fields. A small market town perhaps. Somewhere where she could get a good job and maybe wake up to the sound of birdsong rather than the roar of the city streets, smell fresh air and woodsmoke rather than traffic fumes.

But where did that leave her and Jay? she asked herself bleakly as she fought her way down the steps of the tube station.

Where they were right now. A million miles apart.

Miriam sat in grim contemplation until her stop, and once on the surface again walked home on leaden feet. Her mother had said George was the love of her life. Well, she knew Jay was hers. Without any doubt whatsoever. And she didn't want to live the rest of her life without him, waking up one day to find she was a barren old lady, withered away, grey, wrinkled.

She wanted to love him and trust him and believe in his love for her; she did, so much. But could she? And could she go back to that apartment and take up the sort of life they had shared? And why, *why* hadn't he loved her enough to sweep away all her foolish arguments and demand to see her after he had got back to England? Why, why?

She had been so immersed in her thoughts she didn't notice the car outside the house, so when a car door opened and a voice said, 'Miriam?' she thought for a second she'd imagined Jay into being.

She stared at him through the shadows and he smiled, tawny eyes meeting hers calmly. 'Hi,' he said softly. 'You were miles away.'

Her heart was racing and try as she might she couldn't match his air of quiet self-control. She knew her voice was shaky when she said, 'Hello, Jay.'

He came towards her and she didn't move, a trembling in her stomach causing muscles to clench. He looked gorgeous, big and dark and masculine, his bulky overcoat emphasising the strength and power of his virile attractiveness.

'How are you?' he asked when he reached her, one hand lifting her chin as he kissed her lips in a way that suggested he had every right to do so. 'Mmm.' He drew back a little to look into her eyes. 'You taste of chocolate and wine.'

'It was the office Christmas party,' she answered automatically before realising that that probably wasn't the most tactful reply in view of the events of last year.

Jay nodded. 'Ours too.' He continued to regard her steadily. 'So, how are you?' he said again.

'Fine.' It was a lie and Jay knew it; she could tell from his face. 'How about you?' she added brightly.

'The better for seeing you.'

He could have seen her any time he fancied over the last couple of weeks. Suddenly she wanted to shout at him, to say or do something outrageous to jerk him out of the relaxed, almost nonchalant air he was displaying, but she knew perfectly well she couldn't. He had done nothing wrong after all. He had stayed away because she had made it very plain she required him to. But now he was here she knew that was the last thing she'd wanted. Forcing herself to speak normally, she said, 'How did Germany go?'

'Germany went very well.'

It was faintly mocking and immediately Miriam's hackles rose. It was one thing to lie awake night after night eating her heart out for this man, and quite another for him to stand there making fun of her. 'Good.' She took a step back from him. 'Well, if you'll excuse me I've got things to do. It's going to be an early start tomorrow.'

'Ah, yes, your holiday with Clara. Doesn't Brian mind being left home alone?'

She didn't like him in this mood. Bristling, she snapped, 'Why are you here, Jay?'

'Because I couldn't keep away.' He reached out and took her into his arms, kissing her breath away. Literally. When he raised his head, his eyes glinted down at her. 'And because I wanted to give you your Christmas box.'

'But I haven't got anything for you,' she protested, horrified.

'I've just had what I wanted.' His eye caressed her mouth, making it tingle. 'And don't look so stricken. If you're really concerned, I'll have more of the same later.'

She couldn't do this. She couldn't join in whatever game he was playing. She loved him too much and this was agony. 'Jay, I don't think—'

'Good.' He put a finger to her lips. 'Don't think. This is Christmas. Or nearly. Just go with the magic. Look, I can't give you your present here, and if I come in, ten-to-one the pit bull will be on duty. Come for a ride with me.'

Bewildered, Miriam stared at his shadowed features. The night was bitterly cold, the temperature was dropping by the hour and although her cases were packed she still had a hundred and one last-minute things to do. 'I can't.'

He didn't say anything, he just drew her into his arms again, settling her against the solid bulk of him before kissing her long and deeply. It was a confident kiss, strong and warm, igniting a whole host of emotions she could have done without.

Trying to keep a hold on reality, Miriam said again, 'Really, I can't. You don't understand—'

'Can't is not a word that features in the Carter vocabulary, you know that.' He hadn't let go of her, his breath a white mist in the freezing air. 'I'm only asking for a few minutes, Miriam.' He pressed her closer against him. 'And it is Christmas after all.'

This was crazy, insane. The warning was loud and powerful. But then, could she feel any worse by spending a little time with him than she'd felt over the last days?

His finger outlined her lips, infinitely gentle. 'Please, Miriam. What's ten, fifteen minutes in the overall scheme of things? You'll be back here before you know it.'

'You're sure? Ten minutes?'

'Fifteen at the most.' He kissed the tip of her nose. 'I promise, OK?' Sensing her compliance, he drew her to his car, opening the passenger door for her and helping her in before he walked round the bonnet.

As he slid into the driver's seat Miriam looked at him, at the solid strength of him. His being here tonight meant he still loved and wanted her, didn't it? And she loved and wanted him. When they were together the way they'd been in that hotel room nothing else mattered, not where they lived, their lifestyle, nothing. Almost in spite of herself, she said quietly, 'Why didn't you call me when you got back from the trip?'

He didn't say anything at first, starting the engine and pulling out into the road before he replied. And then it wasn't what she had expected—no 'you told me not to' or 'I thought it was for the best'. Calmly, he said, 'I've been busy.'

Busy? Her hands knotted into fists. *Busy?* 'I see.'

'I doubt it.' He was driving fast, probably too fast, and he didn't look at her when he said, 'Why didn't you call me, Miriam?'

OK, she deserved that one. Because she couldn't answer him, she said, 'Where are we going?'

'Nicely deflected.' The mockery was back but more overt now. 'We're going somewhere quiet, all right?'

He didn't say any more and as the miles and minutes sped by the silence was charged with such raw electricity that Miriam couldn't break it. Eventually, when they had been travelling for a good twenty minutes, she said evenly, 'You said I would be back within fifteen minutes.'

'I lied.'

Her eyes shot to meet his gaze but his profile was impassive as he stared ahead. 'What do you mean, you lied?'

'I lied. I'm not perfect.'

'Jay, this isn't funny.'

'It isn't meant to be.'

For the first time panic reared its head. 'Stop this car; I want to get out.'

'Don't be silly,' he said calmly. 'And relax. You're with me and I wouldn't hurt a hair on your head. It's just time you stopped running, that's all.'

'I order you to stop this car, Jay Carter.'

'Wrong approach, my love.'

It was the 'my love' rather than anything else that stopped her voice, the constriction in her throat painful. It seemed a long time since he had called her that and his use of it now was unbearably poignant.

As the car travelled on in the frosty night, a feeling of unreality took over. Miriam was warm and snug, the icy white world outside the car picturesque and Christmas-card perfect, from the black velvet sky studded with a million twinkling stars to the welcoming lights shining in the windows of the houses they passed. She had ceased to wonder where they were going. She was with Jay. He would keep her safe. She knew that.

When they left the built-up confines of the city for more open territory the powerful car began eating up the miles. It must have been an hour or more from when they'd set off that Jay turned off the country road they had been following for a while. He drove the car between two massive wrought-iron gates which had been secured open, following a wide pebbled drive for a few moments before emerging into a semicircular paved area that led to the steps of a large red-bricked Georgian house.

A tall privet hedge enclosed the front garden, which had been landscaped mainly with dwarf bushes and low shrubbery, but two tall, majestic beech trees stood as sentinels either side of the house. Automatic lights lit up the house and drive, and further illumination came from concealed lighting within the bushes and shrubs.

As Jay came to a halt in front of the house Miriam found her voice. 'Where are we and who lives here?'

Jay turned off the engine and moved to face her, his eyes glittering. 'We're halfway between London and Leamington Spa and a friend of Jayne's lives here. She and her family are spending Christmas with her husband's relations in America and Jayne said she'd keep an eye on the place. Jayne and Guy moved into the area a couple of weeks ago. It's a good place to raise a family.'

Aware she'd asked the wrong questions, Miriam said tightly, 'What I meant was, why are we here?'

'I wanted to show you round.'

'Show me round?' She stared at him in bewilderment. 'But this is someone's house, Jay. You can't just wander in.'

He extracted some keys from his pocket. 'Actually I can,' he said mildly. 'And this front garden is deceptive—there's an acre of ground at the back of the house, including a small orchard.'

She didn't care if there was a full-scale forest, it was someone's private property and regardless of whether Jay had the keys or not it wasn't right to invade Jayne's friend's privacy. Primly, she said, 'I wouldn't dream of taking advantage of this friend's trust in Jayne.'

Jay grinned. 'I've got permission from the owner and her husband, promise.'

'Is that the same sort of promise you made earlier? The fifteen-minute one?'

Jay clapped a hand to his heart. 'You know how to wound.' When she continued to eye him severely, his grin widened. It was terribly sexy. 'Look, I met Bill and Stephanie when I helped Jayne and Guy move—they had us round for a meal the first night. I swear I've got permission, OK? And it's a hell of a drive on a night like this only to sit out in the cold.'

'I don't know…'

'Well, I do.' He slid out of the car and came round to open the passenger door, extending his hand. 'Come on.'

This was *crazy*. What on earth was she doing miles from home on a cold, frosty night when she'd got to be up at the crack of dawn tomorrow?

Strong hands persuaded her out of the car and once she was standing he held her hand as he led her up the steps to the front door. It wasn't a big deal, it wasn't even particularly intimate, but the feel of his fingers holding hers caused Miriam to be overwhelmed by a flood of mixed emotions. She didn't understand where this was going but suddenly the feeling she'd experienced in the car returned. She was with Jay and he wouldn't hurt her.

He opened the door and then stood aside for her to enter the house first after turning on the light and punching a number into the alarm located on the wall. The action was reassuring. She didn't feel so much of an intruder now.

The large hall was beautiful, the natural wood floor relieved by a couple of handsome rugs and the light walls and ceiling in perfect harmony with the mellow wood. Jay led her into a vast kitchen first, then a smaller utility room that was still bigger than her bedsit. A breakfast room, dining room, enormous sitting room and second reception room along with a very adequate study made up the ground floor, but when Miriam entered the main sitting room she stopped dead. Jay had left this room till last and when she looked at the enormous log fire crackling in the walk-in fireplace and the nine-foot Christmas tree—a vision of gold and red—in a corner with gaily wrapped parcels beneath it, she felt panic hit. 'Jay, someone's here. They must be back.'

'Relax, Bill and Stephanie aren't back until well into the New Year but someone *is* staying here over Christmas. Us.'

'Us?' she repeated vacantly.

'Us. You and me. The two of us.' He pulled her into him, encircling her waist and drawing her close. 'And I promise it's with their blessing.'

She had gone rigid in his arms. 'I can't stay here.'

'You can,' he soothed. 'It's all arranged. This is a trial run to see if you like the place. The family's moving to America next year and they want to sell.'

She stared at him wildly. 'I'm going on holiday with Clara tomorrow.'

'You were going on holiday with Clara tomorrow,' he corrected very gently. 'But now Brian's going instead. And your suitcases and all the things Clara thought you might need are in one of the bedrooms upstairs.'

'Clara?' She couldn't take it in. 'Clara wouldn't do this to me.' She jerked herself free and he let her go, watching her with inscrutable eyes. 'She's my friend.'

'Which is precisely why she *did* do it. She wants the best for you and that's me,' he said with a complete lack of modesty. 'Everyone thinks so, including your mother.'

Part of her couldn't believe this was happening. The other part acknowledged it had the Carter stamp all over it. 'You're mad,' she said faintly.

'Probably, where you're concerned. Madly in love and always will be, but we weren't getting anywhere with the softly-softly approach.'

'But you don't like Clara and she doesn't like you.' It was probably a silly thing to say in the circumstances but Jay only smiled.

'When I called her on my return from Germany we had a very interesting chat,' he said calmly. 'I had to revise my opinion of her and I think she did the same with me. Certainly she's been very helpful over the last week or two with all the arrangements and so on. As has your mother, of course. Lovely woman, your mother, and there are not too many men who can say that and mean it about their mother-in-law. I took them both out for a meal one night—'

'Clara and my mother? You took Clara and my *mother* out?'

'And we pooled notes. The result was very interesting. We decided my plan was perfect,' he continued serenely as though she hadn't spoken.

'You charmed them.' She could see it all. But she had thought Clara was made of sterner stuff.

'They love you,' he said, suddenly very serious. 'And without any prompting from me they both agreed you need me. Not as much as I need you probably, but then that would be impossible. And living apart wasn't helping you to come to terms with anything. I agree it would be difficult for us to both live in your bedsit, and there was no way you were coming back to the apartment—I've got that up for sale, incidentally—and a hotel room over Christmas wasn't my idea of togetherness. And so I had a word with Bill and Stephanie and they were delighted to think their home would be of use. Whether we buy it or not is incidental. I haven't even suggested that to them as yet.'

'You're selling the apartment?' She hadn't heard past that. The apartment was the prize that proclaimed how far he had come, his jewel in the crown, his triumph. 'But you love it.'

'It's an apartment, Miriam.' His eyes were very steady as they held hers. 'That's all. And one thing I've learned over the last twelve months is that home is where you are. It's that simple.'

As she stared at him she became aware for the first time that he wasn't as cool and composed as he would like her to believe. A small muscle in his jaw gave away the iron control in which he was holding himself. He wasn't sure how she was going to react, she realised with a start of surprise. He was nervous. It melted her more than anything else could have done.

All she had done for the last year was push him away. Even when she had come to believe that the affair with Belinda was just a product of the other woman's thwarted desire, she had still pushed him away.

And all he had done was love her.

'I'm also selling part of the business.' Again his voice was matter-of-fact. 'Cutting back on the workload. If I never did another day's work in my life I'd still have more than enough money to keep us very comfortably off, but I couldn't sit around twiddling my thumbs all day; I'm not made that way. But I realise there's a fine line between me driving the business and the business driving me, and I want to make sure I'm around for the things that really matter. So the property side of Carter Enterprises is going.'

'What are the things that really matter?' she whispered faintly.

'You. Us. Our life together. Kids. Building a family home.'

She could barely see him for the tears she couldn't hold at bay a moment longer. 'But I'm such a mess,' she suddenly wailed, surprising them both. 'And I'd got it all wrong about my mother, she—she told me—'

'I know, I know.'

Somehow she was in his arms and he was stroking her hair, his voice deep and soft as he soothed her sobs.

'And I want to trust you, I do, I do, but what if I can't? You—you'll grow to hate me—'

'Never.'

'And I don't feel I fit into your world with the dinners and parties and everyone thinking you should have married someone different.' She hiccuped loudly. 'And they do. Your friends and business colleagues.'

'If they do, which I doubt, they're wrong.' He mopped her face with a crisp white handkerchief, his touch infinitely gentle. 'It's us that matters, only us. Here…' He undid her coat and slipped it off her shoulders, doing the same with his and flinging them on a sofa. Then he picked her up in his arms and carried her over to a big plumpy armchair close to the fire, settling her on his lap and kissing her.

'Listen to me,' he said quietly, brushing the tears from her cheeks with his thumbs. 'We both made mistakes.'

'No, it was me.'

'We both made mistakes,' he repeated firmly. 'I expected you to slide into my life without giving you credit for the pressures it imposed. *My* apartment, *my* friends, *my* social and work life. I had no idea you felt the way you did about the apartment and at first I blamed you for not telling me, I admit it. But then I asked myself if I'd ever given you the chance. It was all cut and dried, wasn't it? When two people marry they form a new life together, set up home, establish their own group of friends, but instead I carried on exactly as before but with the addition of a wife.'

'I—I didn't mind that.' She sniffed. 'Not most of the time anyway, not at first. It was only later, but by then we were—oh, I don't know. In a pattern, I suppose.'

'A pattern that needed to be broken.' He kissed her again, holding her so closely she could feel the steady beat of his heart. 'We're going to start again, my love. Build a new foundation and this time we'll do it right. We'll work through your insecurities a day at a time but from this minute onwards we bare our souls to each other, nothing kept back. I'm going to spend more time with you and you're going to talk to me, really talk because I can't guess what's gong on in that mind of yours. I'm only a man.'

She whispered something, so softly he bent his head as he said, 'What's that?'

'I'm—I'm frightened you'll be disappointed with me.' It was another fear from the past. Her father had been so disappointed with her and her mother that he had walked. She had carried that through her childhood and for a long time afterwards, even when she had come to realise that it was nothing to do with herself and her mother, that her father was a vain, shallow wastrel who would never be much use to any woman.

'Impossible.' He brushed his mouth slowly over hers. 'I love you, Miriam. Everything about you, all the facets of your personality and character that make up the whole. Your softness, your warmth, your sense of humour, your vulnerability—they're all precious because they add up to the final you. And don't ask me why you're so utterly special, why if I can't have you I'd shrivel up and die inside, because I don't know except to say that's what the mystery of true love is all about.'

He lifted his hand to her face, the tawny eyes blazing with such love she knew it was real, for ever, that she was seeing the soul of him. A wonder rose up in her, filling her with indescribable joy.

'Do you love me?' he asked very seriously.

Miriam nodded. 'More than you can imagine,' she murmured tremulously.

'And will you live with me in a home we start together, somewhere where children can fill up all the empty corners?'

Her fingers came gently to his mouth, tracing the firm

contours of his lips. 'Yes,' she whispered, and he heaved an unsteady breath.

'My darling,' he said huskily, 'we're going to have a wonderful Christmas.'

CHAPTER ELEVEN

WHEN Miriam awoke on Christmas Eve she was aware of being cocooned in a delicious cosy warmth, but it was only when she opened her eyes she realised she wasn't in her little bedsit. Jay was beside her and she was lying curled into his body with her back to his chest, his muscled, hairy leg entwined intimately with hers and one of his large hands holding the soft mound of her breast. From his steady, deep breathing she knew he was fast asleep.

She didn't know what time it was but the weak winter sunlight filtering through the partly drawn curtain told her it wasn't early. Which wasn't surprising in view of the fact that they hadn't gone to sleep until dawn.

She shut her eyes again and lay relaxed and still in the comfort of the big bed, her mind reliving the hours of lovemaking they'd indulged in. He had undressed her slowly in front of the roaring fire in the sitting room at first as they had whispered sweet nothings to each other in an orgy of love, divesting himself of his own clothes before drawing her down onto the thick lambswool rug in front of the fire. He had touched and tasted her with sensual tenderness for a long time until she had begun to tremble with frustration, and when he had taken her her body had been fluid, every nerve-ending responding to the satin-hard invader inside her.

They had eaten a supper of champagne and caviar snuggled together and wrapped in an enormous fleecy throw Miriam recognised as coming from the apartment, the glow from the fire and the lights from the Christmas tree throwing mellow flickering shadows over the dark room.

Later Jay had carried her up the winding staircase to their bedroom stark naked, the two of them laughing and caressing and teasing like a pair of teenagers.

The bedroom suite was gorgeous, decorated in pale greens and lilac with a large *en suite* and the most enormous bed, and Miriam was enchanted to see a real fire burning in the ornate fireplace. Once nestled in the soft covers, Jay had spent all night showing her how much he had missed her, their lovemaking enhanced by the truths they had whispered to each other downstairs. For the first time she was allowing herself to believe the fairy tale could come true and it was intoxicating, washing away the last of her inhibitions and giving her the courage to meet him kiss for kiss, caress for caress with an abandon she hadn't displayed before. They had drifted off to sleep only as it grew light, large, fat flakes of snow falling outside the window.

A white Christmas. It had been her last conscious thought before she had slept and now she hugged it to her, unable to believe she was really here, with Jay, in this beautiful house for the holidays. And her mother and Clara conspiring together! She smiled to herself. It really was the season of miracles.

Jay moved slightly in his sleep, his hand on her breast tightening for a moment before relaxing again. She wanted to see his face and she tried to slowly turn but their bodies were entwined in such a way she was locked beneath him.

He shifted again and she took the opportunity to manoeuvre herself round as his leg lifted slightly before once again settling over hers. She stared at him, drinking her fill of his sleeping face, relaxed and calm and so boyish. Once he was awake a slight cynicism and hardness that the years had brought firmed his mouth and made the faint lines radiating from his eyes more pronounced, but like this he was all hers.

She caught at the thought, mentally shaking her head at herself. He *was* all hers, awake or asleep. She had to trust in this forever love. Too many nights in the past when they had been first married she had lain like this watching him sleep, tormenting herself with imagining how many other women had done the same. Beautiful, glamorous, exciting women. Women who still remained out there, a constant threat. But Jay didn't want anyone else, she knew that now. She didn't know why he loved her the way he did because she was remarkably unexceptional, but he did, and that was all that mattered.

She shut her eyes tightly, saying a little prayer of thankfulness that he hadn't given up on her, that he had loved her enough to weather the storm and steer their boat into calm waters. When she opened them again he was staring straight at her, his beautiful tawny eyes smiling.

'Good morning, Mrs Carter.' He nuzzled her ear before kissing her neck. 'You smell delicious, better than any breakfast.'

'So do you.' With his black hair tousled over his forehead and the sexiest stubble darkening his chin, he *looked* even better.

'I had the most incredible dreams.' His voice was still husky with sleep. 'I dreamt we made love till dawn.'

She smiled. Pressed close to him, she could feel his hard arousal. 'But then you woke up,' she teased softly.

'That I did.' He rolled over, supporting himself by his elbows as he lay across her, the tip of his masculinity touching her most intimate place. He began to shift a few inches back and forth as he ruffled the tight curls at the V of her thighs, causing every muscle in her body to tighten.

He pushed slightly, entering her just the tiniest bit, and she gasped, exquisite ripples of sensation causing her abdomen to contract.

'Every morning is going to start like this.' He kissed her open mouth, his body continuing to play with hers. He wasn't rushing her, the slow sensuality building as he used his skill to heighten her responses. Only when she was at fever-pitch did he possess her completely, her internal muscles contracting so violently that they provided his release too.

It was a while before their bodies finally became still, and even then Miriam continued to tremble in the aftermath of passion. Jay cradled her to him, kissing her nose, her eyes, her forehead with tiny, burning kisses before finally taking her mouth.

Their joining had been intense and almost painfully poignant. A year today she had woken up wanting to die, to just go to sleep and never wake up, believing she had lost him.

'There has never been anyone but you and there never will be.' He had read her mind with that remarkable way he had. 'Do you believe that, Miriam? Are you there yet?'

She was learning not to be surprised at his intuition. 'I think so,' she whispered shakily. 'I want to believe it.'

'You will.' His voice rang with assurance. 'You're mine in the same way I'm yours. It's actually very simple.'

She nodded, her head against his chest, a wave of emotion threatening to consume her. He was so strong, so sure. If she couldn't trust her own feelings of fear and vulnerability, perhaps she could trust Jay? It was a new slant on things and one that made sense. She clung to him, needing his strength and love. For the first time she realised she could let go and be herself, that he wouldn't condemn her for her fears but would shoulder them with her.

Tremblingly, she murmured, 'I do trust you, Jay. I'm beginning to realise it's Miriam Carter I'm not sure about. The more I try to analyse the past the more I realise what a mess I've made of things.'

'Not really.' He took her face in his hands. 'When I talked with your mother she was the first to admit she'd made a big mistake in not discussing your father leaving with you. It left a void in which all kinds of misunderstanding could grow. She did it absolutely for the best at the time but she told me you both struggled in the early days when money was very tight and you had no real home. Your father sent no maintenance and did nothing to help her, but it wasn't that she minded so much. It was his ability to cut his own flesh and blood out of his life. If that hurt her it must have hurt you too.'

Miriam nodded. She had always felt it was a weakness and almost a betrayal of her mother to mind that her father was gone, to miss him, but the child she had been then *had* minded. And to cover up the hurt and sense of rejection she had told herself she hated and despised him. She'd told herself that so often it had become true. 'I used to wonder what was wrong with me that my own father didn't want me,' she admitted slowly. 'I think I even thought that if they hadn't had me then he would have stayed with my mother and they'd have been happy, like they must have been before I was born.'

He kissed away her tears, hugging her to him. 'But you don't think like that any more?'

She shook her head. 'Not after talking with my mother.'

'And you accept he was flawed? That he couldn't really love anyone but himself? There are men and women like that out there, sweetheart, and it was just unfortunate your mother got involved with one when she was so young and naive.'

'I know.'

'But our children will know what it is to have two parents who love each other and them,' he said tenderly, 'and that's what you focus on in the future. Our home will be a place with no secrets, no skeletons in cupboards. We'll give them a foundation of truth and trust to build their lives on.'

Her arms tightened around him. 'I love you,' she whispered, her voice husky with love.

'And I you.' He kissed her again, hard and passionately, before sitting up in bed. 'And I hate to bring things down to a more mundane level but I'm so hungry I could eat a horse.'

She smiled at his rueful face. 'I presume in all this planning you've been doing you stocked the fridge and freezer?'

'Oh, yes.' He grinned complacently. 'And there's plenty of champagne and wine to see us over the Christmas break. I've thought of everything.'

She didn't doubt it.

'We'll eat and then I'll show you the rest of the house and the grounds.' He slid out of bed, reaching for one of the two thick, fleecy robes which again Miriam recognised from the apartment, throwing it to her before pulling on his own. 'Come on, woman,' he said teasingly, 'into the kitchen where you belong.'

The next few days were heaven on earth. The house was wonderful and even before she'd seen each room Miriam had agreed they would put in an offer to Jayne's friends.

Once Jay knew she had fallen in love with the magnificent old house he admitted the couple who owned it were looking to move out soon, the husband having just been told he'd secured a terrific job in the States close to his elderly parents, who were beginning to get quite frail.

Christmas Eve afternoon they spent making a family of snowmen in the garden like two excited children, returning to the warmth of the house as the sun set in a river of red and gold, turning the tranquil, frosted-pearl sky into a blaze of breathtaking colour.

That night they made love again before falling asleep in each other's arms, sated and happy, waking up on Christmas Day to the sound of church bells and more snow. The trees in the grounds at the back of the house were a Christmas-card wonderland and they stood wrapped in each other's arms once again, gazing out into the wintry beauty for some time before having breakfast and then walking to the small parish church for the Christmas service.

Jay had bought her heaps of presents, which he'd piled around the tree. Some were silly, funny gifts to make her laugh—a pair of Rudolph slippers with massive red noses that bobbed when she walked and a Father Christmas hat that sang 'When Santa Got Stuck up the Chimney' when you pressed the pompom on the top of the hat. Others, like the sexy black underwear and finely wrought gold and diamond bracelet, were more expensive. Miriam phoned her mother to wish her a happy Christmas and the two of them laughed and cried together, promising they would all get together for a meal very soon.

Boxing Day they spent in bed, a day of pure indulgence, the need inside them raging and overpowering. Miriam found she couldn't get enough of Jay and she knew he felt the same. The taste, the smell, the feel of him was all-important to her, and she found it hard to believe she'd managed to get through the last twelve months without being able to run her hands over his hard body and sleep curled close into his warmth each night.

Jayne and Guy called by the day after Boxing Day, inviting them to a New Year's Eve party they were holding so they could meet all the neighbours. Jayne was already looking prettily pregnant and the pair of them were touchingly proud of the small, compact mound in her stomach.

Miriam had wondered how Jay's sister would be with her when they met again but she needn't have worried. It was as if they had only seen each other the day before.

'Come early on New Year's Eve,' Jayne said as they hugged goodbye on the doorstep. 'I want to show you the baby's room. We've decorated it in cream and yellow—I didn't want to know whether it was a boy or a girl.' She wrinkled her small nose. 'I said to Guy I want a surprise at the end of all the hard work.'

'I don't blame you,' said Miriam, laughing, and silently blessing Jay's sister for her sunny, forgiving nature. It would be lovely to live so close to them.

New Year's Eve was crisply cold and frosty, and as Miriam got ready for the party she was thankful she had splashed out on a couple of new cocktail dresses for the proposed holiday with Clara. The silk-mix red dress strewn with pearls brought out the highlights in her chestnut hair, and with Jay's bracelet on her wrist and simple diamond studs in her ears she felt elegant for once.

Jay whistled admiringly as he zipped her into the dress. 'You look a million dollars,' he murmured softly, dropping a swift kiss on the back of her neck. She'd looped her hair on top of her head, leaving a few wispy curls to soften the style, and now he wound a tendril around one finger, adding, 'But I prefer you in that gorgeous birthday suit of yours.'

Miriam giggled. 'I think Jayne and Guy might have something to say if I turned up at their party stark naked to meet the neighbours, don't you?'

'You could still wear my bracelet.'

'Of course. Why didn't I think of that?'

The snow had gradually dispersed in the meagre warmth of a winter sun over the last two or three days, although evidence of it still remained where snow ploughs had banked masses at the side of roads, and their family of snowmen in the garden were still there, albeit just formless lumps now. Jayne and Guy's house being a fifteen-minute walk away, they decided not to take the car.

It was late afternoon when they left, wrapped up warmly against the bitter cold. Jack Frost had already been hard at work and a glittering coating of white adorned the bare branches of trees and bushes, creating a carpet of diamond dust on the ground. There had been another magnificent sunset earlier, but now the night sky was a soft indigo, the fragrance of burning leaves and woodsmoke in the still air.

This was almost too beautiful, too perfect. As Miriam held tightly to Jay's arm and looked up at the star-studded sky she felt a moment's fear prick her happiness before she told herself not to be so silly. They were together again and they loved each other. Nothing could get in the way of that.

Jayne and Guy's house was a large semi-detached Victorian property in the heart of the small village near by, and after Jayne had shown her the baby's room and Miriam had oohed and ahhed over the collection of tiny vests, sleeping suits and other paraphernalia they went downstairs to join the two men, who were sitting in front of the fire with a drink in their hands. Jay slipped his arm around her as she sat down beside him and Guy poured her a glass of wine, Jayne wrinkling her nose at the orange juice she had been drinking since her pregnancy had been confirmed. 'Not that I mind really,' she added quickly—as though anyone had doubted that.

They spent a pleasant hour until the first of the guests began to arrive and soon the party was going with a swing. The neighbours turned out to be a pleasant group of people on the whole, and Miriam was just laughing at something one of Jayne's old university friends had said—a rather zany girl who was eight months pregnant and reminded her of Clara, but with a bump—when she glanced across the room as the latest guests arrived.

The smile froze on her face. She blinked, but the tall blonde woman hanging on the stout older man's arm remained. Not an hallucination, then. Belinda Poppins really was standing there as large as life, looking absolutely marvelous in a skin-tight black dress with a plunging neckline that ended in a gather at her waist.

'Wow.' Clara with a bump followed her gaze. 'She's got some nerve, even with the modern miracle of invisible tape. Still, if you've got it, flaunt it. Isn't that what they say?'

She must have made some reply, although she didn't

know what. Jay was talking to a young couple on the other side of the room and as she looked across at him he glanced up and caught her gaze, smiling before his face straightened as he took in her expression. Instinctively her eyes went back to Belinda and as he followed the direction she was looking she saw him become very still for a moment. Then he was making his way towards her, his tawny eyes intent on her white face.

'I didn't know.' As he reached her he took her arm, pulling her into him with his back to the rest of the room, so shielding her. 'I had absolutely no idea Jayne knew her; to my knowledge she's never met her. You believe me, don't you?'

She nodded, unable to speak.

'And Jayne wouldn't have invited her if she knew who she was anyway. It must be the man she's with that's the contact.'

Miriam nodded again.

'I can't believe it; of all the things to happen.' He swore softly under his breath, still holding her tight.

Whether it was Jay's obvious distress or her new-found belief and trust in him which had steadily grown over the last little while, Miriam didn't know, but suddenly her mind started to work again. Reaching up, she touched his face. 'It doesn't matter,' she said quietly. 'She can't hurt us any more, Jay. Her lies are useless now.'

'We'll go.'

'No.' Her stomach was turning over with the shock of seeing the woman who had caused them such heartache but at the same time she felt something strange bubbling up. She didn't know if it was thankfulness or relief or even joy, but it was all to do with the knowledge that, seeing Belinda again like this, she knew, without a shadow of a doubt, that

Jay hadn't betrayed her with this woman. How could she have thought it for one moment? she asked herself in amazement. Belinda looked what she was, a beautiful, cold, poisonous snake, shallow and without morals. And Jay? Jay was fine and good and honest. Even if he had been physically attracted to Belinda, which she didn't think was the case, he wouldn't have done anything about it, loving her, his wife, as he did. When Jay had asked her to be his wife and had stood beside her and said his vows before God and man he had meant them for life. She had known that then or she wouldn't have married him and she knew it now—how could she have lost that confidence during the time in between? But never again.

'No?' He looked down into her face, willing her to be honest with him about how she was feeling.

'Jay, I love you and I trust you.' It probably wasn't the place to make the declaration, it perhaps ought to have been said after they had made love or looking at a beautiful sunset or something equally romantic, but it was the right time none the less. 'And I believe in you absolutely. All the Belindas in the world can't impinge on us, I know that now. So we'll stay as long as we want to, although I've no plans to become her new best friend.'

He didn't smile and a long pause ensued, their eyes locked. She willed him to see what was in hers. Finally he reached out and touched her cheek, one tender stroke of the backs of his fingers down her soft skin. 'I love you,' he said so softly she was almost reading his lips. 'So much.'

'I know.' She felt giddy with emotional release, the room spinning for a moment as she held on to him. 'And I love you.'

She saw him release a breath and then he did smile, pure

relief showing on his face. 'Some New Year's Eve, eh? I'll make sure it's better next year.'

'This year's just fine.'

It was a little while before their paths crossed with that of Belinda's; Jay's ex-secretary had clearly been trying to avoid them. She was holding on to the arm of her escort and, close to, Miriam realised the man was older than she'd initially thought—sixty if a day. The gold Rolex on his wrist and the expensive suit he was wearing suggested he wasn't short of a penny or two, though.

Jay smiled thinly at the man but Belinda he surveyed in stony silence, his eyes as hard as amber.

It was Miriam who spoke first. 'Hello, Belinda.' She turned her gaze on the man, smiling as she said, 'I don't think we've been introduced.'

Belinda's escort's eyes had narrowed—he'd clearly sensed something was amiss—but he held out his hand. 'Graham Martyn,' he said cordially. 'We're staying with my daughter, Kate Rowan, for a couple of days.'

'I'm sorry, we're new to the area,' Miriam said carefully.

'But you know Belinda?' He half turned to the woman at his side, who hadn't said a word.

With some effort, Belinda said shortly, 'I used to work for Jay.'

'Oh, yes?' Graham looked at Jay, who stared back at him unblinkingly. 'When was that?'

'A year ago,' Jay said in a tone in which ice tinkled.

'Just before you came to work for me.' Again Graham was looking at Belinda, but now his voice was quiet and even. 'I thought you'd been taking a sabbatical for the couple of years preceding that? Travelling? Seeing a little of the world? Wasn't that why your references were out-of-date?'

Jay made a sound in his throat. No one could have mis-understood the derision. 'This is not the time or the place,' he said, the softness of his voice coated with steel, 'but if you'd care to ring me in the New Year I'd be happy to tell you why Miss Poppins had no current reference. Jay Carter of Carter Enterprises.'

'I know the name.' Graham Martyn nodded. 'I might just do that, Mr Carter.'

Still Belinda said nothing; she clearly didn't dare to take Jay on in the mood he was in. Miriam didn't blame her. She almost felt sorry for the woman. Almost, but not quite. If Belinda had had her way she would have destroyed their marriage. Even when she must have realised there was no chance with Jay, sheer spite had driven her on.

Graham and Belinda left shortly afterwards, and as soon as they had gone Jayne made her way to their sides, her eyes curious. 'I saw you talking to Graham,' she said in a loud whisper. 'Did you know the woman he's with? Poor Kate's going out of her mind with worry. She's sure that woman's angling to become the next Mrs Martyn and all the family can't stand her. She's a total gold-digger but she's playing him like a violin apparently.'

'Not for much longer.' Jay told his sister who Belinda was, causing Jayne to look at Miriam in horror.

'Miriam, I'm so sorry. I never knew. I wouldn't have dreamt of letting her into the house. Oh, I can't believe this has happened, not just when you two have got back together.'

'It's fine, truly.' Miriam patted Jayne's arm. 'She did her worst but we survived it and we're all the stronger for it. Isn't that so, Jay?'

He tucked her hand in his arm. 'I wanted to strangle her,' he admitted wryly.

Miriam laughed. She was feeling light-headed with happiness and she had only had one glass of wine all evening, wanting to keep a clear head in view of Belinda's presence.

It was then that the knowledge hit her. Mentally calculating, she wondered how the absence of her monthly cycle hadn't registered before. But there had been so much happening.

That first Monday in December when they had gone to the hotel. She blinked, her heart racing as the noise and laughter around her faded away. And now she was three weeks late. And the odd little feeling of giddiness she'd had in the last few days, and this morning she hadn't felt too good first thing, although it had swiftly passed...

Could it be? Her hand went protectively over her stomach. But she was, she knew she was. She felt different. She was expecting Jay's baby.

Two days later Jay came home to the apartment to find a bright-eyed wife and a candle-lit dinner waiting for him. They had agreed it made sense to stay in the apartment until they could move into the house, which hopefully would happen within two months, their offer having been accepted. Miriam didn't mind the apartment now— wherever Jay was was home.

'This is very nice.' He had kissed her until she was breathless as soon as he had walked through the door. 'What are we celebrating? Not our first day back at work surely?'

'Something better than that.'

'I should hope so.'

He took the glass of champagne she had waiting for him, his brow furrowing when she lifted up her glass of orange juice.

'A toast.' Her voice was light, joy-filled. 'To you.'

'Me?' He smiled, amused. 'On orange juice?'

'To you,' she said solemnly, looking straight into the tawny eyes she loved so much. 'And this.' She held up the little tube she'd purchased from the chemist that day. 'You're going to be a father, Jay. We're expecting a baby.'

The next minute she was in his arms, champagne and orange juice spilling onto the floor as he lifted her right off her feet with a whoop of delight, twirling her round and round before he kissed her until the whole world shifted. But when it righted again he was there. As he was always to be.

* * * * *

The debt, the payment, the price!

A ruthless ruler and his virgin queen. Trembling with
the fragility of new spring buds, Ionanthe will go to
her husband. She was given as penance, but he'll
take her for pleasure!

Harlequin Presents® is delighted to unveil an
exclusive extract from Penny Jordan's new book
A BRIDE FOR HIS MAJESTY'S PLEASURE

PEOPLE WERE PRESSING in on her—the crowd was carrying her along with it, almost causing her to lose her balance. Fear stabbed through Ionanthe as she realized how vulnerable she was.

An elderly man grabbed her arm, warning her, 'You had better do better by our prince than that sister of yours. She shamed us all when she shamed him.'

Spittle flecked his lips, and his eyes were wild with anger as he shook her arm painfully. The people surrounding her who had been smiling before were now starting to frown, their mood changing. She looked around for the guards, but couldn't see any of them. She was alone in a crowd that was quickly becoming hostile to her. She hadn't thought it was in her nature to panic, but she was beginning to do so now.

Then Ionanthe felt another hand on her arm, in a touch that extraordinarily her body somehow recognized. And a familiar voice was saying firmly, 'Princess Ionanthe has already paid the debt owed by her family to the people of Fortenegro. Her presence here today as my bride and your princess is proof of that.'

He was at her side now, his presence calming the crowd

and forcing the old man to release her as the crowd began to murmur their agreement to his words.

Calmly but determinedly Max was guiding her back through the crowd. A male voice called out to him from the crowd. 'Make sure you get us a fine future prince on her as soon as may be, Your Highness.'

The sentiment was quickly taken up by others, who threw in their own words of bawdy advice to the new bridegroom. Ionanthe fought to stop her face from burning with angry humiliated color. Torn between unwanted relief that she had been rescued and discomfort about what was being said, Ionanthe took refuge in silence as they made their way back toward the palace.

They had almost reached the main entrance when once again Max told hold of her arm. This time she fought her body's treacherous reaction, clamping down on the sensation that shot through her veins and stiffening herself against it. The comments she had been subjected to had brought home to her the reality of what she had done; they clung inside her head, rubbing as abrasively against her mind as burrs would have rubbed against her skin.

'Isn't it enough for you to have forced me into marrying you? Must you force me to obey your will physically, as well?' she challenged him bitterly.

Max felt the forceful surge of his own anger swelling through him to meet her biting contempt, shocking him with its intensity as he fought to subdue it.

Not once during the months he had been married to Eloise had she ever come anywhere near arousing him emotionally the way that Ionanthe could, despite the fact that he had known her only a matter of days. She seemed to delight in pushing him—punishing him for their current situation, no doubt, he reminded himself as his anger subsided. It was completely out of character for him to let anyone get under his skin enough to make him react emotionally when his response should be purely cerebral.

'Far from wishing to force you to do anything, I merely wanted to suggest that we use the side entrance to the palace. That way we will attract less attention.'

He had a point, Ionanthe admitted grudgingly, but she wasn't going to say so. Instead she started to walk toward the door set in one of the original castle towers, both of them slipping through the shadows the building now threw across the square, hidden from the view of the people crowding the palace steps. She welcomed the peace of its stone interior after the busyness of the square. Her dress had become uncomfortably heavy and her head had started to ache. The reality of what she had done had begun to set in, filling her with a mixture of despair and panic. But she mustn't think of herself and her immediate future, she told herself as she started to climb the stone steps that she knew from memory led to a corridor that connected the old castle to the more modern palace.

She had almost reached the last step when somehow or other she stepped on the hem of her gown, the accidental movement unbalancing her and causing her to stumble. Max, who was several steps below her, heard the small startled sound she made and raced up the stairs, catching her as she fell.

If she was trembling with the fragility of new spring buds in the wind, then it was because of her shock. If she felt weak and her heart was pounding with dangerous speed, then it was because of the weight of her gown. If she couldn't move, then it was because of the arms that imprisoned her.

She had to make him release her. It was dangerous to be in his arms. She looked up at him, her gaze traveling the distance from his chin to his mouth and then refusing to move any farther. What had been a mere tremor of shock had now become a fiercely violent shudder that came from deep within her and ached through her. She felt dizzy, light-headed, removed from everything about herself she considered 'normal' to become, instead, a woman who hungered for something unknown and forbidden.

* * * * *

Give yourself a present this Christmas—
pick up a copy of
A BRIDE FOR HIS MAJESTY'S PLEASURE
by Penny Jordan,
available December 2009 from Harlequin Presents®!

HARLEQUIN Presents

Bestselling Harlequin Presents author

Penny Jordan

brings you an exciting new book:

A BRIDE FOR HIS MAJESTY'S PLEASURE

A ruthless ruler and his virgin queen.

Trembling with the fragility of new spring buds,
Ionanthe will go to her husband. She was given as
penance, but he'll take her for pleasure!

Book #2876

**Give yourself a present this Christmas—
pick up a copy of
A Bride for His Majesty's Pleasure
by Penny Jordan.**

*Available December 2009
from Harlequin Presents®*

EXTRA

INNOCENT WIVES

Powerful men—ready to wed!

They're passionate, persuasive and don't
play by the rules…they make them!

And now they need brides.

But when their innocent wives say "I Do," can it ever
be more than a marriage in name only?

Look out for all our exciting books this month:

Powerful Greek, Unworldly Wife #81
by SARAH MORGAN

Ruthlessly Bedded, Forcibly Wedded #82
by ABBY GREEN

Blackmailed Bride, Inexperienced Wife #83
by ANNIE WEST

The British Billionaire's Innocent Bride #84
by SUSANNE JAMES

Wild, Wealthy and Wickedly Sexy!

We can't help but love a bad boy!

The wicked glint in his eye…the rebellious streak
that's a mile wide. His untamed unpredictability.
The way he'll always get what he wants, on his
own terms. The sheer confidence, charisma and
barefaced charm of the guy.…

In this brand-new miniseries from
Harlequin Presents, these heroes have
all that—and a lot more!

DEVIL IN
A DARK BLUE SUIT
by **Robyn Grady**

Book #2881

Available December 2009

REQUEST YOUR FREE BOOKS!

2 FREE NOVELS PLUS 2 FREE GIFTS!

YES! Please send me 2 FREE Harlequin Presents® novels and my 2 FREE gifts (gifts are worth about $10). After receiving them, if I don't wish to receive any more books, I can return the shipping statement marked "cancel." If I don't cancel, I will receive 6 brand-new novels every month and be billed just $4.05 per book in the U.S. or $4.74 per book in Canada. That's a savings of close to 15% off the cover price! It's quite a bargain! Shipping and handling is just 50¢ per book*. I understand that accepting the 2 free books and gifts places me under no obligation to buy anything. I can always return a shipment and cancel at any time. Even if I never buy another book, the two free books and gifts are mine to keep forever.

106 HDN EYRQ   306 HDN EYR2

Name	(PLEASE PRINT)	
Address		Apt. #
City	State/Prov.	Zip/Postal Code

Signature (if under 18, a parent or guardian must sign)

Mail to the **Harlequin Reader Service**:
IN U.S.A.: P.O. Box 1867, Buffalo, NY 14240-1867
IN CANADA: P.O. Box 609, Fort Erie, Ontario L2A 5X3

Not valid to current subscribers of Harlequin Presents books.

Are you a current subscriber of Harlequin Presents books and want to receive the larger-print edition? Call 1-800-873-8635 today!

* Terms and prices subject to change without notice. Prices do not include applicable taxes. Sales tax applicable in N.Y. Canadian residents will be charged applicable provincial taxes and GST. Offer not valid in Quebec. This offer is limited to one order per household. All orders subject to approval. Credit or debit balances in a customer's account(s) may be offset by any other outstanding balance owed by or to the customer. Please allow 4 to 6 weeks for delivery. Offer available while quantities last.

Your Privacy: Harlequin Books is committed to protecting your privacy. Our Privacy Policy is available online at www.eHarlequin.com or upon request from the Reader Service. From time to time we make our lists of customers available to reputable third parties who may have a product or service of interest to you. If you would prefer we not share your name and address, please check here. ☐

HP09R

HARLEQUIN *Presents*

TWO CROWNS, TWO ISLANDS, ONE LEGACY

A royal family torn apart by pride and its lust for power, reunited by purity and passion

THE ROYAL HOUSE *of* KAREDES

Harlequin Presents is proud to bring you the last three installments from The Royal House of Karedes. You won't want to miss out!

THE FUTURE KING'S LOVE-CHILD
by Melanie Milburne, December 2009

RUTHLESS BOSS, ROYAL MISTRESS
by Natalie Anderson, January 2010

THE DESERT KING'S HOUSEKEEPER BRIDE
by Carol Marinelli, February 2010

Darkly handsome—proud and arrogant
The perfect Sicilian husbands!

DANTE: CLAIMING HIS SECRET LOVE-CHILD
by
Sandra Marton

The patriarch of a powerful Sicilian dynasty,
Cesare Orsini, has fallen ill, and he wants atonement
before he dies. One by one he sends for his sons—
he has a mission for each to help him clear his
conscience. His sons are proud and determined,
but the tasks they undertake will change
their lives forever!

Book #2877

Available November 24, 2009

Look for the next installment
from Sandra Marton coming in 2010!

www.eHarlequin.com

HP12877